STONE ARCH BOOKS

a capstone imprint

STONE ARCH BOOKS™

Published in 2012
A Capstone Imprint
1710 Roe Crest Drive
North Mankato, MN 56003
www.capstonepub.com

Originally published by DC Comics in the U.S. in single magazine form as Superman Adventures #1.

DC Comics
1700 Broadway, New York, NY 10019
A Warner Bros. Entertainment Company

Printed in the United States of America
in North Mankato, Minnesota
032018 000289

Cataloging-in-Publication Data is available at the Library of Congress website:
ISBN: 978-1-4342-4549-6 (library binding)

Summary: Angry over Superman's destruction of his Lex Skel 5000 battle suit, Luthor creates a Superman android to take his revenge on the real Man of Steel.

STONE ARCH BOOKS

Ashley C. Andersen Zantop *Publisher*
Michael Dahl *Editorial Director*
Donald Lemke & Sean Tulien *Editors*
Heather Kindseth *Creative Director*
Bob Lentz *Designer*
Kathy McColley *Production Specialist*

DC COMICS

Mike McAvennie *Original U.S. Editor*
Bruce Timm *Cover Artist*

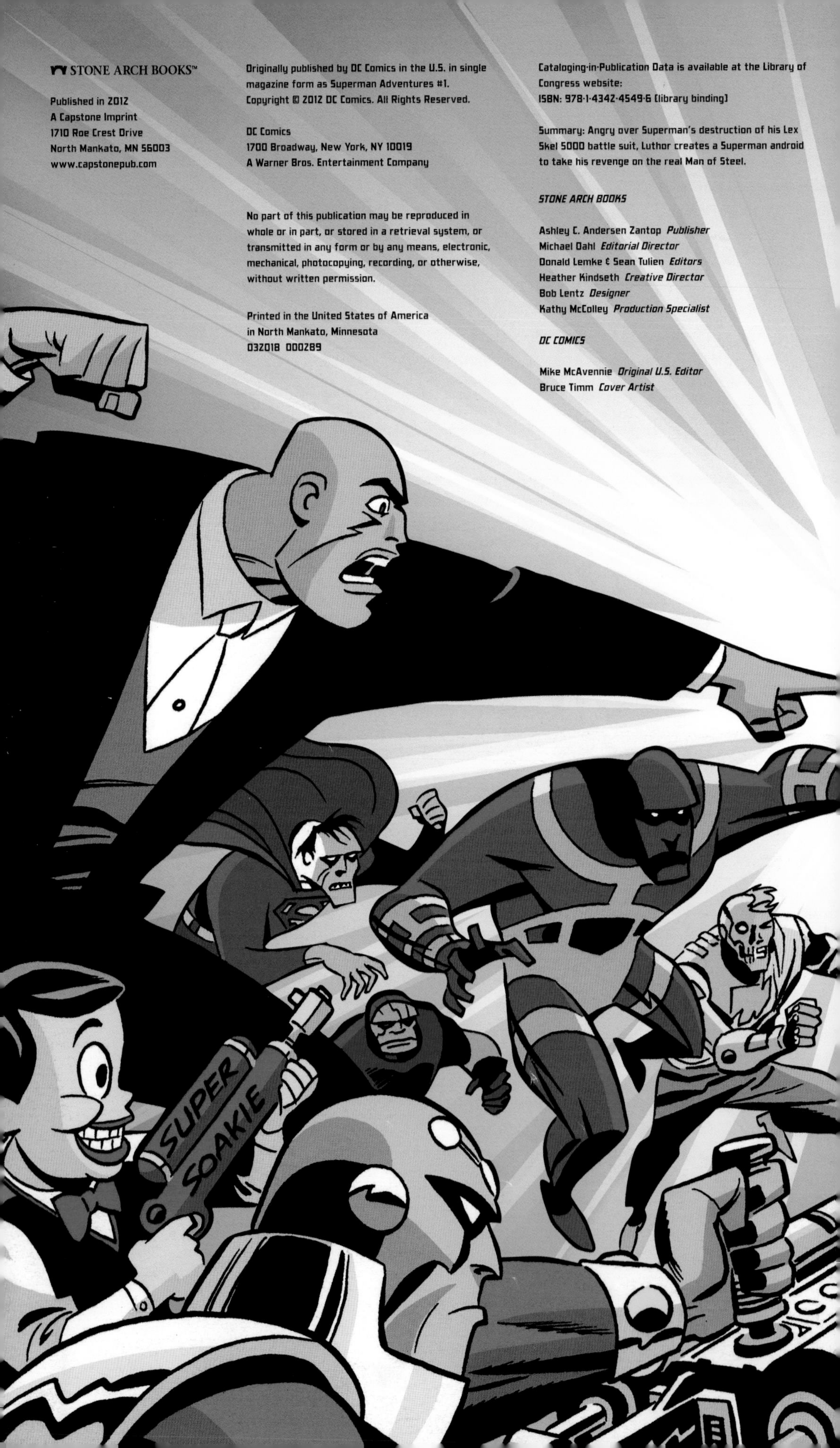
SUPER
SOAKIE

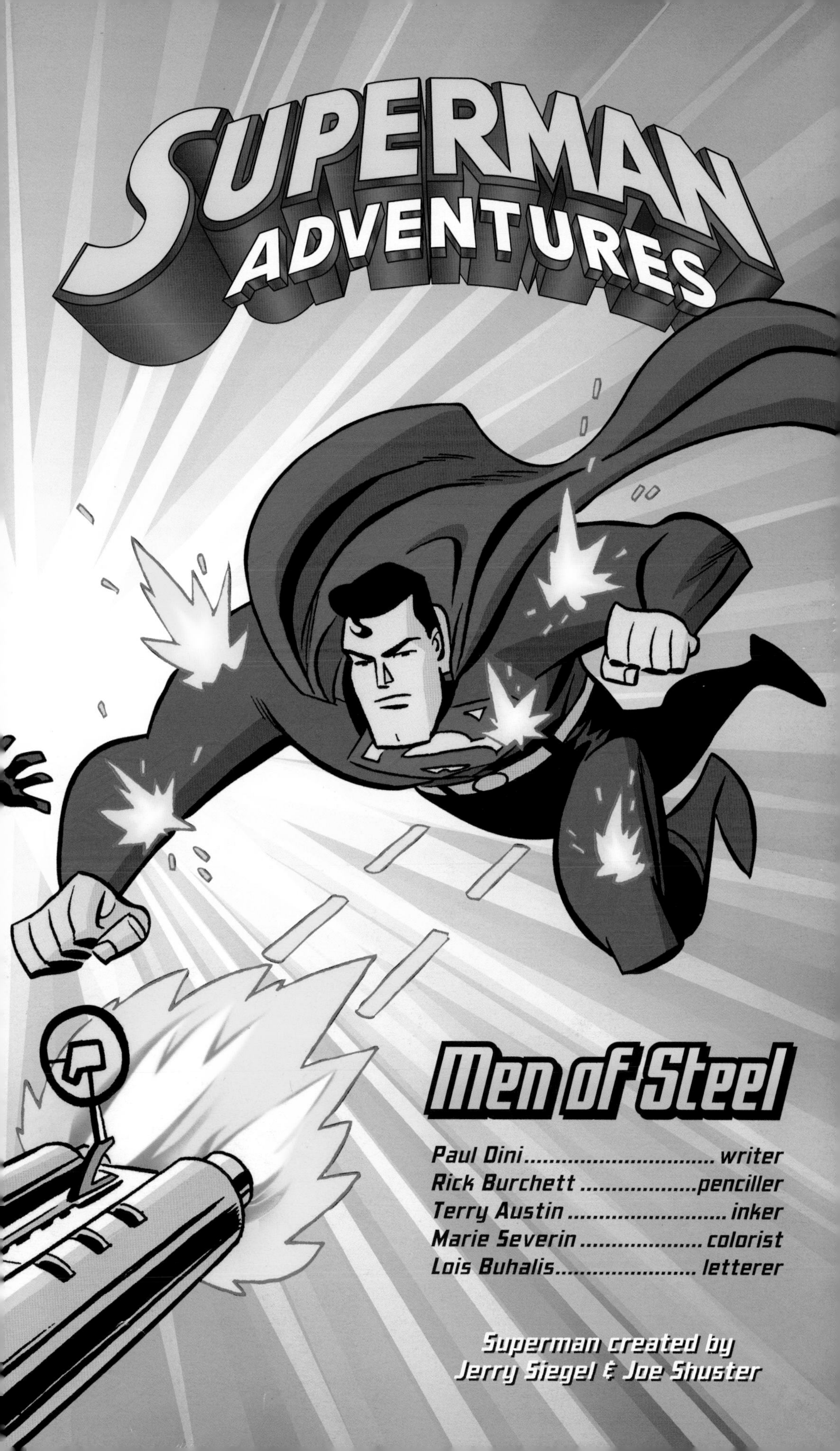

SUPERMAN ADVENTURES

Men of Steel

Paul Dini................................ writer
Rick Burchett ....penciller
Terry Austin .... inker
Marie Severin .... colorist
Lois Buhalis....................... letterer

Superman created by
Jerry Siegel & Joe Shuster

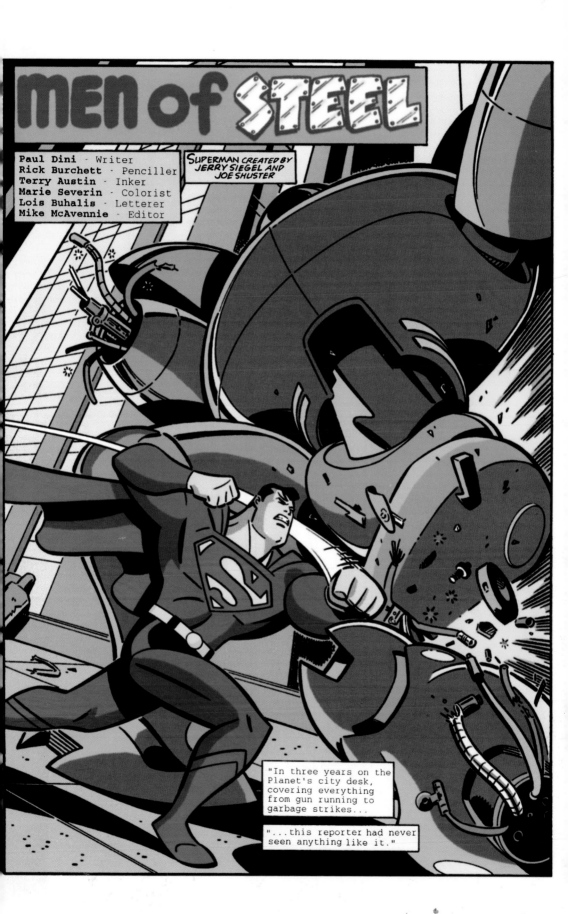

MEN of STEEL

Paul Dini - Writer
Rick Burchett - Penciller
Terry Austin - Inker
Marie Severin - Colorist
Lois Buhalis - Letterer
Mike McAvennie - Editor

SUPERMAN *CREATED BY JERRY SIEGEL AND JOE SHUSTER*

"In three years on the Planet's city desk, covering everything from gun running to garbage strikes...

"...this reporter had never seen anything like it."

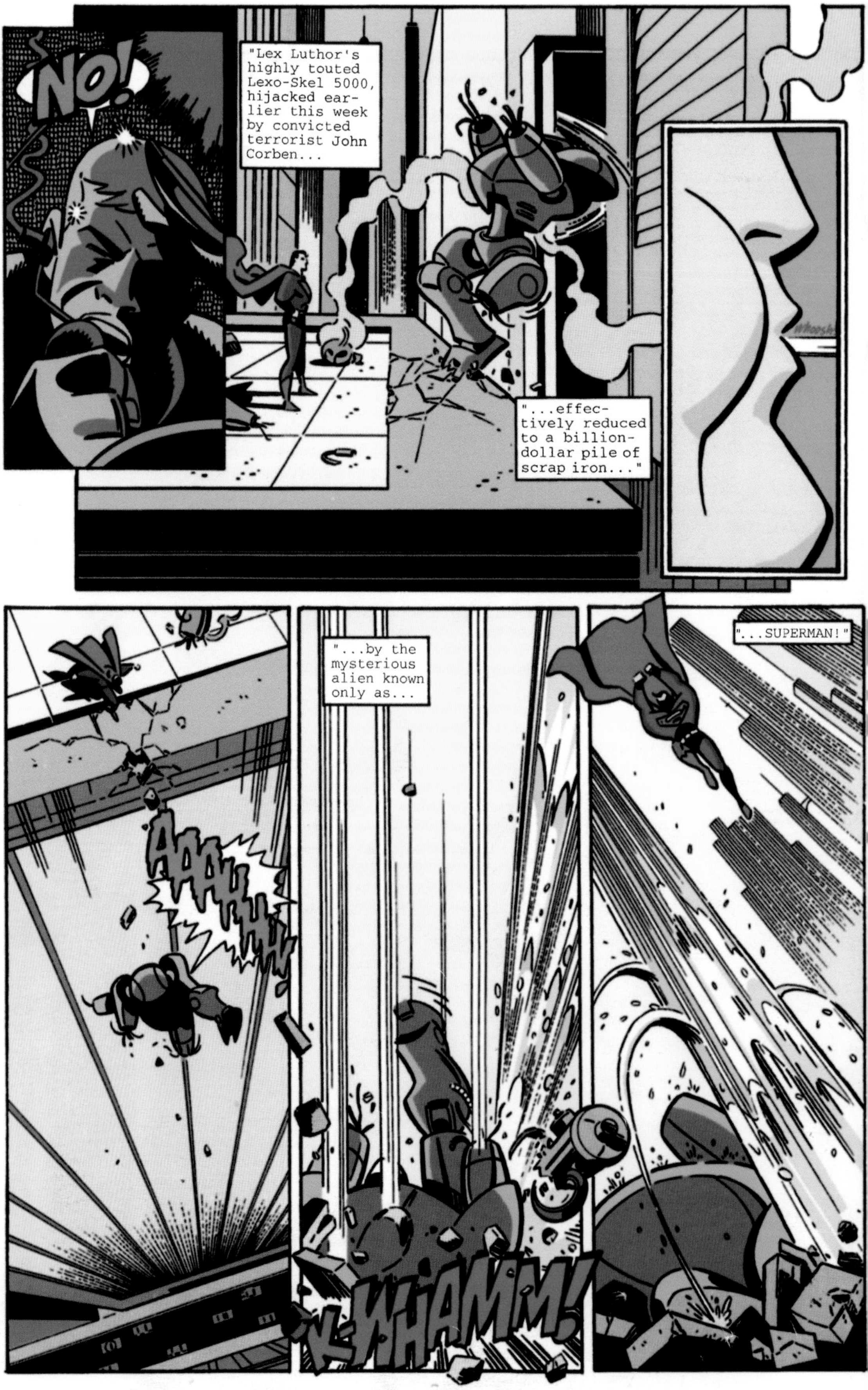
NO!
"Lex Luthor's highly touted Lexo-Skel 5000, hijacked ear-lier this week by convicted terrorist John Corben...
"...effec-tively reduced to a billion-dollar pile of scrap iron..."
AAAHHH
"...by the mysterious alien known only as...
K-WHAMM!
"...SUPERMAN!"

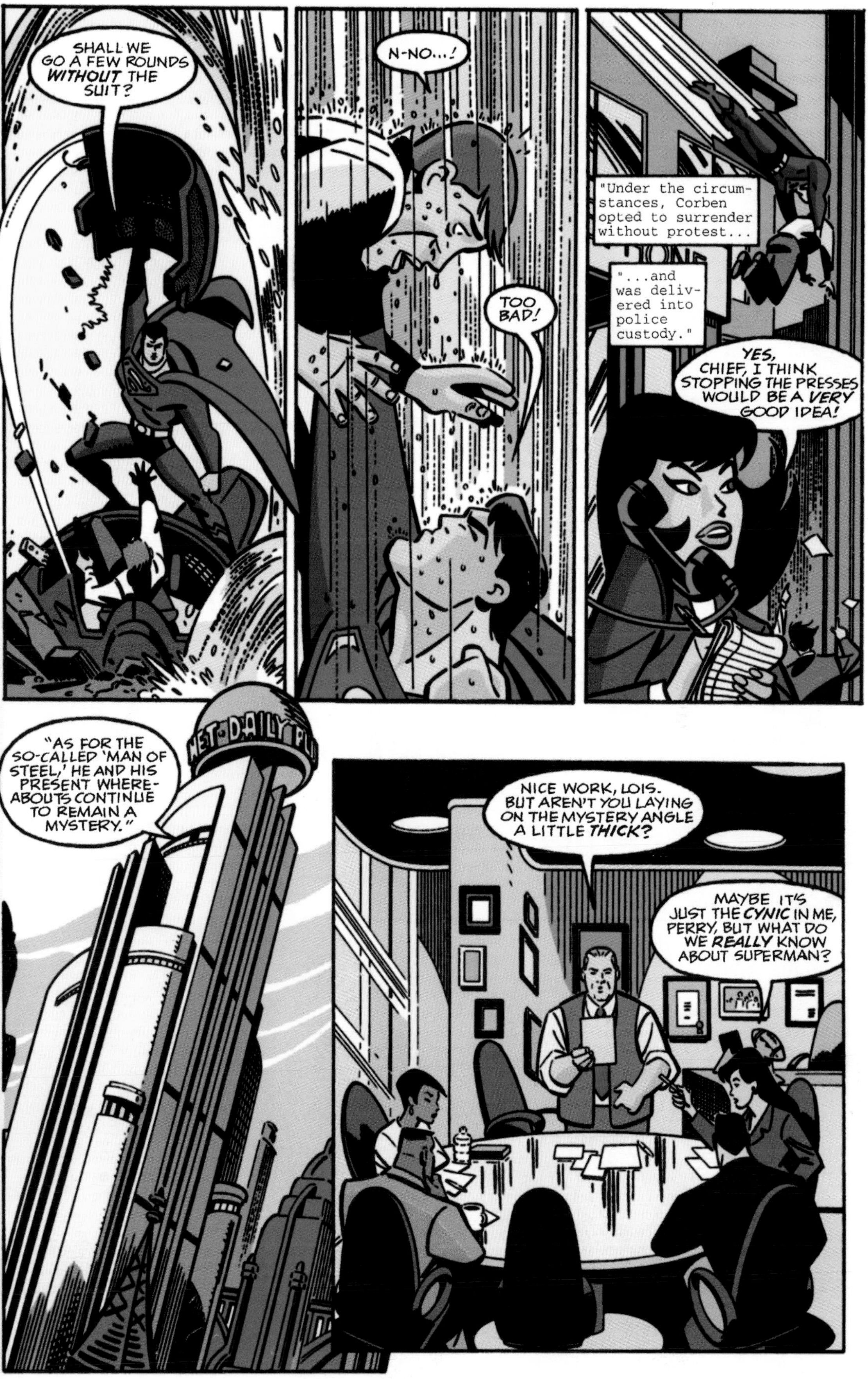
SHALL WE GO A FEW ROUNDS WITHOUT THE SUIT?
N-NO...!
TOO BAD!
"Under the circumstances, Corben opted to surrender without protest...
"...and was delivered into police custody."
YES, CHIEF, I THINK STOPPING THE PRESSES WOULD BE A VERY GOOD IDEA!
"AS FOR THE SO-CALLED 'MAN OF STEEL,' HE AND HIS PRESENT WHEREABOUTS CONTINUE TO REMAIN A MYSTERY."
NICE WORK, LOIS. BUT AREN'T YOU LAYING ON THE MYSTERY ANGLE A LITTLE THICK?
MAYBE IT'S JUST THE CYNIC IN ME, PERRY, BUT WHAT DO WE REALLY KNOW ABOUT SUPERMAN?

SURE, HE *SEEMS* TO HAVE EVERYONE'S BEST INTERESTS AT HEART, BUT AS A REPORTER, I NEVER TAKE *ANYONE* AT FACE VALUE...

...ESPECIALLY IF THEY CAN *FLY!*

CAN'T BLAME YOU THERE. WHAT ABOUT YOU, RON? ANGELA?

I THINK IF SUPERMAN HAD AN ULTERIOR MOTIVE, WE'D HAVE SEEN IT BY NOW, CHIEF. HE'S ONLY BEEN IN TOWN A FEW DAYS AND ALREADY HE'S SAVED DOZENS OF LIVES.

THE GUY'S *DEFINITELY* FOR REAL.

YOU CAN SAY THAT AGAIN! SUPERMAN'S THE HOTTEST STORY TO HIT METROPOLIS IN YEARS!

I'M RUNNING EYEWITNESS ACCOUNTS IN MY COLUMN, PLUS EXCLUSIVE FOOTAGE OF THE BIG GUY IN ACTION ON TONIGHT'S "METROPOLIS EDITION."

AND I GOT SOME GREAT SHOTS OF HIM PUTTING OUT THAT FIRE LAST NIGHT IN SUICIDE SLUM!

I COULD LET YOU HAVE THEM IN EXCHANGE FOR, *OH,* I DUNNO, A *JOB* ON THE PHOTO STAFF?

YOU NEVER QUIT, *DO* YOU, OLSEN?

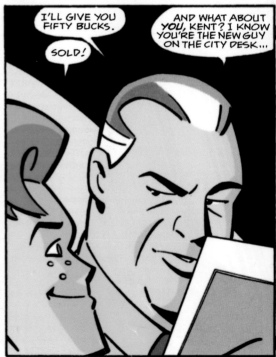

I'LL GIVE YOU FIFTY BUCKS.

SOLD!

AND WHAT ABOUT *YOU,* KENT? I KNOW YOU'RE THE NEW GUY ON THE CITY DESK...

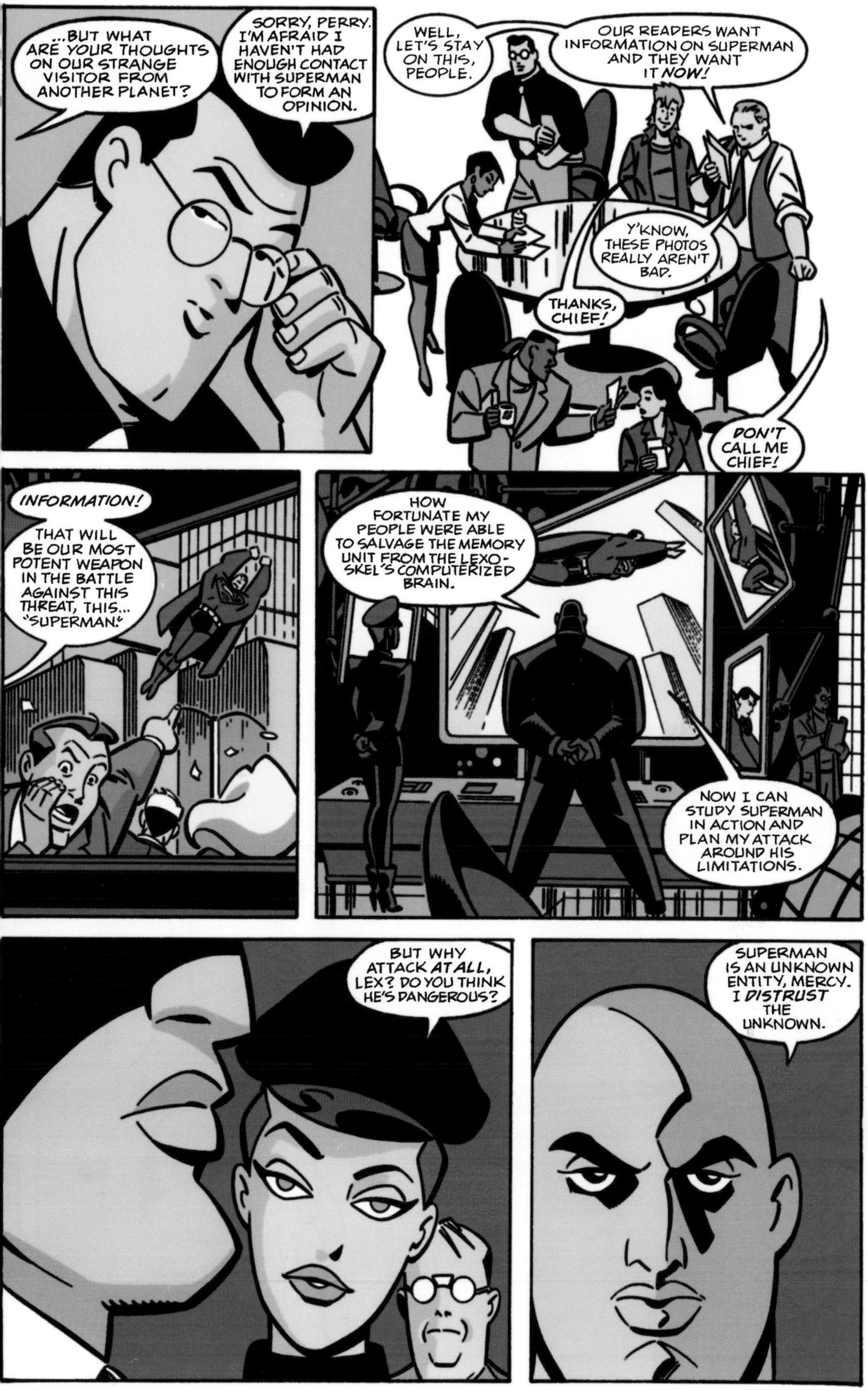
...BUT WHAT ARE YOUR THOUGHTS ON OUR STRANGE VISITOR FROM ANOTHER PLANET?
SORRY, PERRY. I'M AFRAID I HAVEN'T HAD ENOUGH CONTACT WITH SUPERMAN TO FORM AN OPINION.
WELL, LET'S STAY ON THIS, PEOPLE.
OUR READERS WANT INFORMATION ON SUPERMAN AND THEY WANT IT NOW!
Y'KNOW, THESE PHOTOS REALLY AREN'T BAD.
THANKS, CHIEF!
DON'T CALL ME CHIEF!
INFORMATION!
THAT WILL BE OUR MOST POTENT WEAPON IN THE BATTLE AGAINST THIS THREAT, THIS... "SUPERMAN."
HOW FORTUNATE MY PEOPLE WERE ABLE TO SALVAGE THE MEMORY UNIT FROM THE LEXO-SKEL'S COMPUTERIZED BRAIN.
NOW I CAN STUDY SUPERMAN IN ACTION AND PLAN MY ATTACK AROUND HIS LIMITATIONS.
BUT WHY ATTACK AT ALL, LEX? DO YOU THINK HE'S DANGEROUS?
SUPERMAN IS AN UNKNOWN ENTITY, MERCY. I DISTRUST THE UNKNOWN.

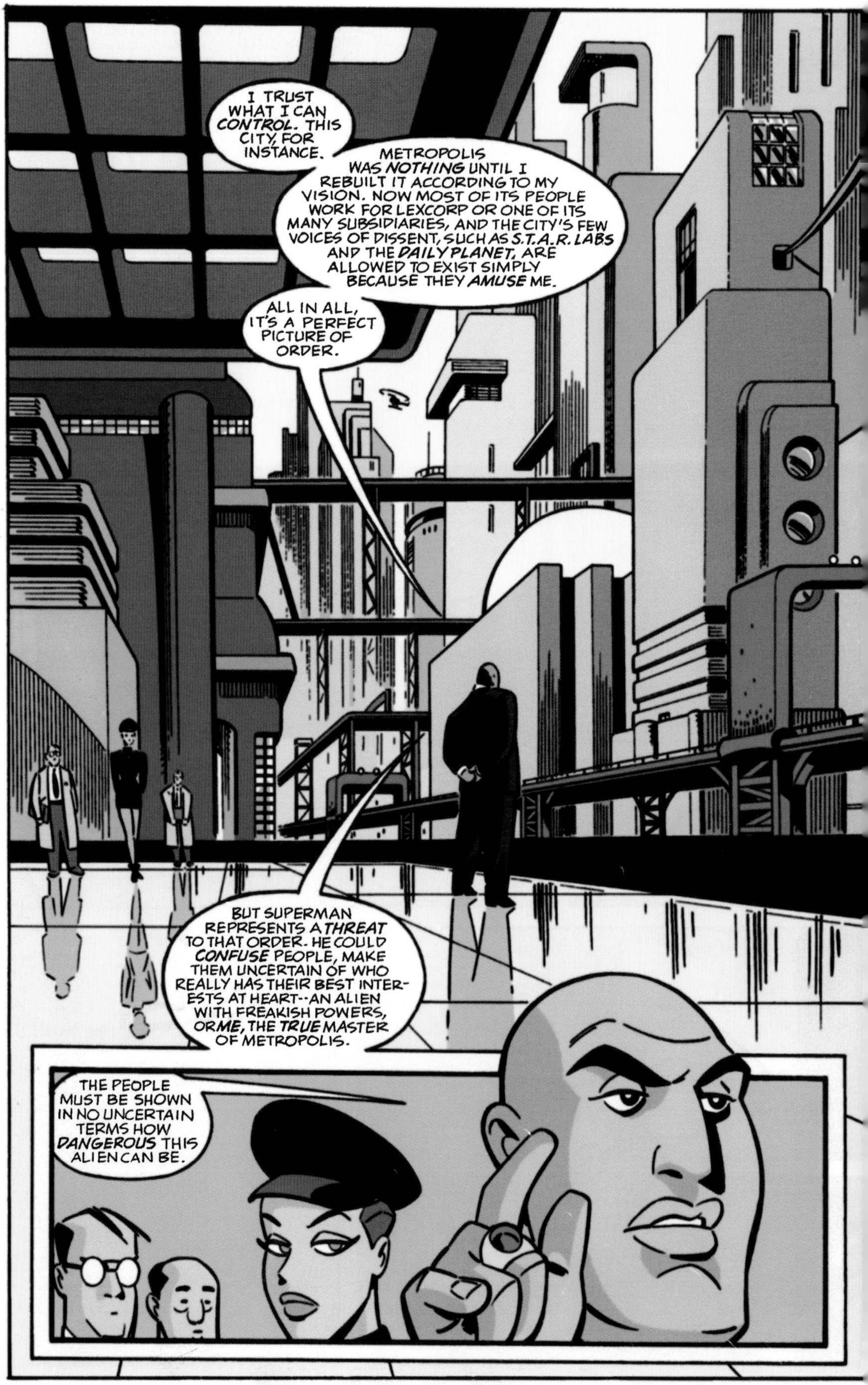
I TRUST WHAT I CAN CONTROL. THIS CITY, FOR INSTANCE.
METROPOLIS WAS NOTHING UNTIL I REBUILT IT ACCORDING TO MY VISION. NOW MOST OF ITS PEOPLE WORK FOR LEXCORP OR ONE OF ITS MANY SUBSIDIARIES, AND THE CITY'S FEW VOICES OF DISSENT, SUCH AS S.T.A.R. LABS AND THE DAILY PLANET, ARE ALLOWED TO EXIST SIMPLY BECAUSE THEY AMUSE ME.
ALL IN ALL, IT'S A PERFECT PICTURE OF ORDER.
BUT SUPERMAN REPRESENTS A THREAT TO THAT ORDER. HE COULD CONFUSE PEOPLE, MAKE THEM UNCERTAIN OF WHO REALLY HAS THEIR BEST INTER-ESTS AT HEART--AN ALIEN WITH FREAKISH POWERS, OR ME, THE TRUE MASTER OF METROPOLIS.
THE PEOPLE MUST BE SHOWN IN NO UNCERTAIN TERMS HOW DANGEROUS THIS ALIEN CAN BE.

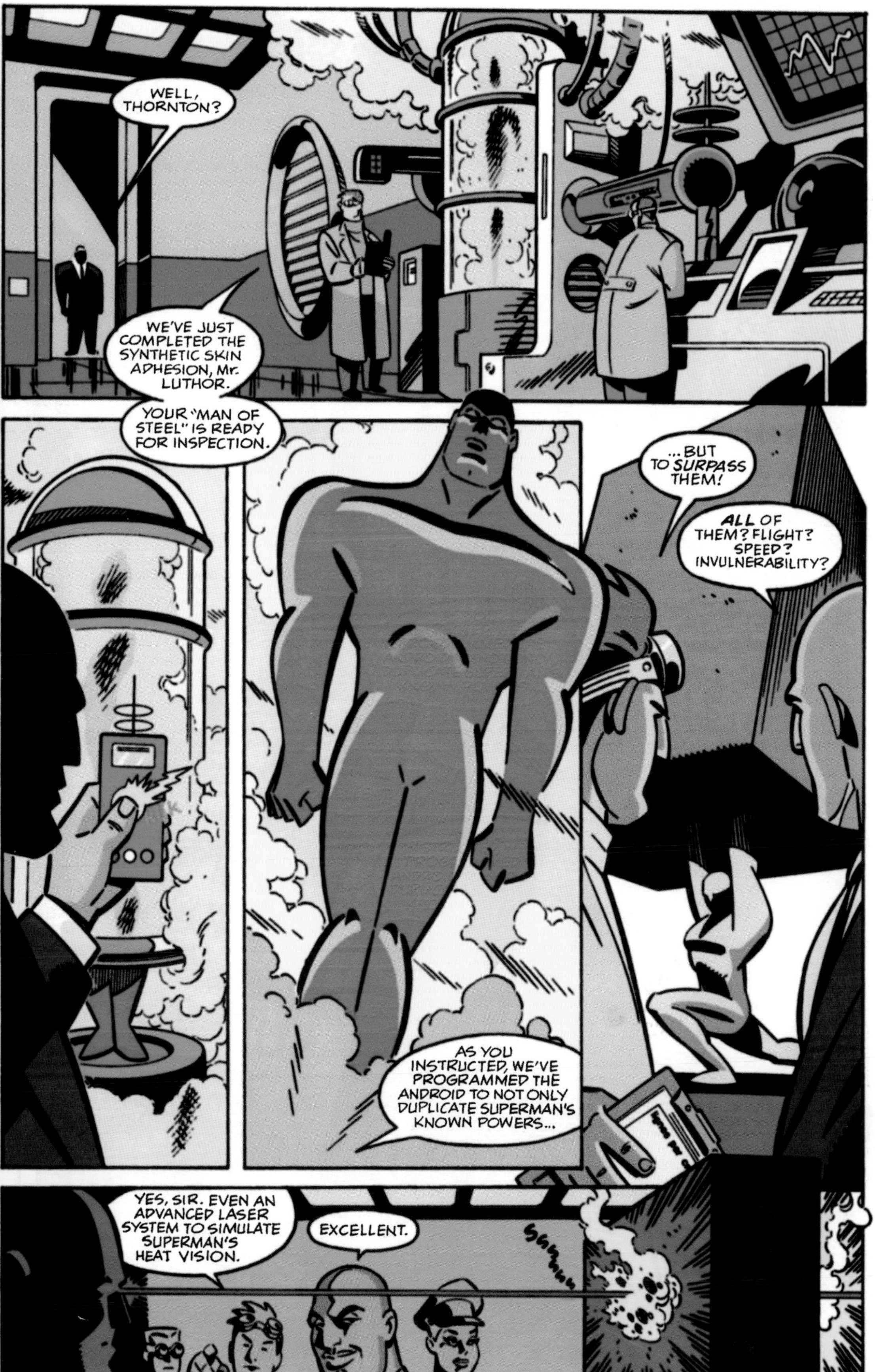
WELL, THORNTON?
WE'VE JUST COMPLETED THE SYNTHETIC SKIN ADHESION, Mr. LUTHOR.
YOUR "MAN OF STEEL" IS READY FOR INSPECTION.
AS YOU INSTRUCTED, WE'VE PROGRAMMED THE ANDROID TO NOT ONLY DUPLICATE SUPERMAN'S KNOWN POWERS...
...BUT TO SURPASS THEM!
ALL OF THEM? FLIGHT? SPEED? INVULNERABILITY?
YES, SIR. EVEN AN ADVANCED LASER SYSTEM TO SIMULATE SUPERMAN'S HEAT VISION.
EXCELLENT.

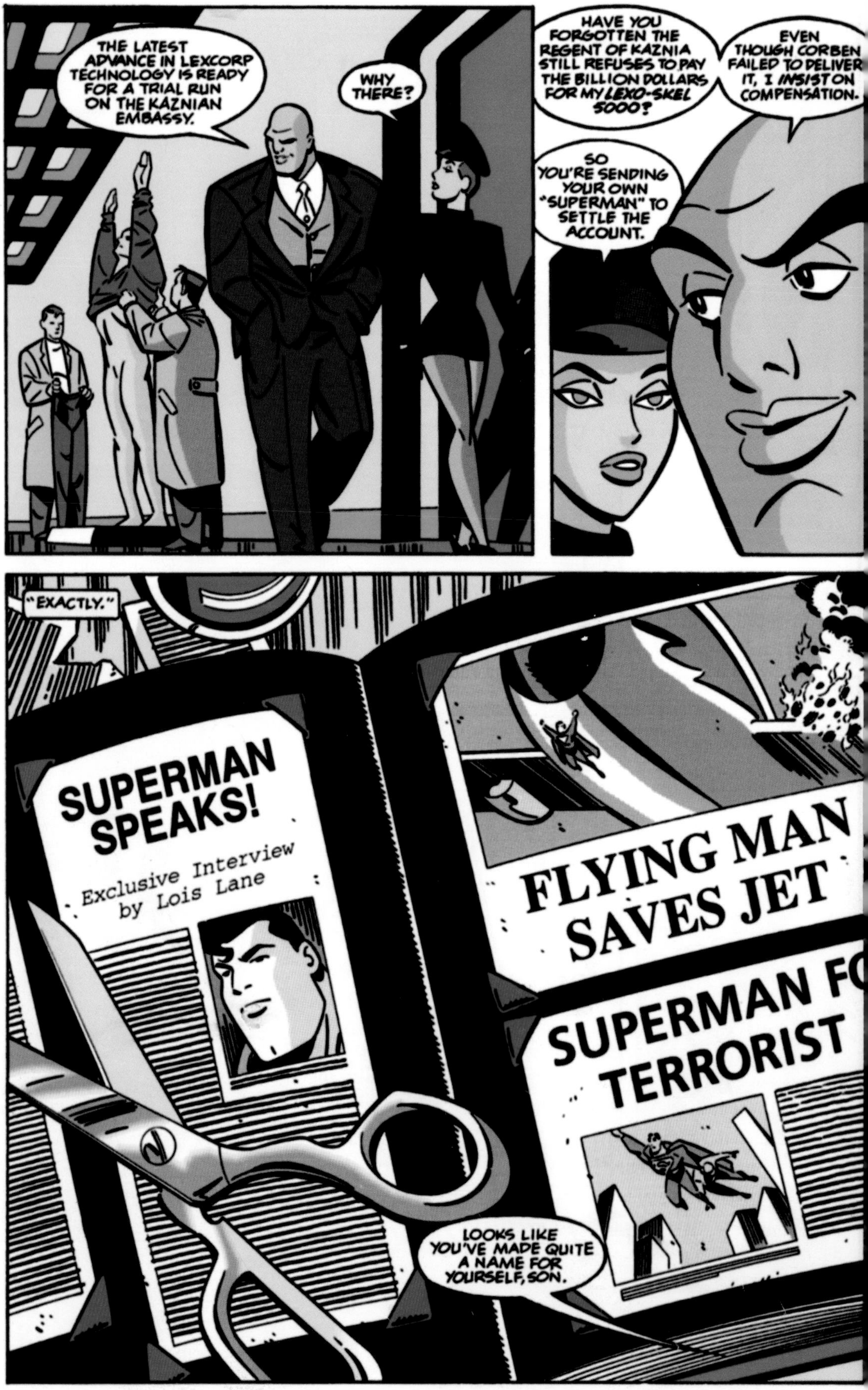
THE LATEST ADVANCE IN LEXCORP TECHNOLOGY IS READY FOR A TRIAL RUN ON THE KAZNIAN EMBASSY.
WHY THERE?
HAVE YOU FORGOTTEN THE REGENT OF KAZNIA STILL REFUSES TO PAY THE BILLION DOLLARS FOR MY LEXO-SKEL 5000?
EVEN THOUGH CORBEN FAILED TO DELIVER IT, I INSIST ON COMPENSATION.
SO YOU'RE SENDING YOUR OWN "SUPERMAN" TO SETTLE THE ACCOUNT.
"EXACTLY."
SUPERMAN SPEAKS!
Exclusive Interview by Lois Lane
FLYING MAN SAVES JET
SUPERMAN FO
TERRORIST
LOOKS LIKE YOU'VE MADE QUITE A NAME FOR YOURSELF, SON.

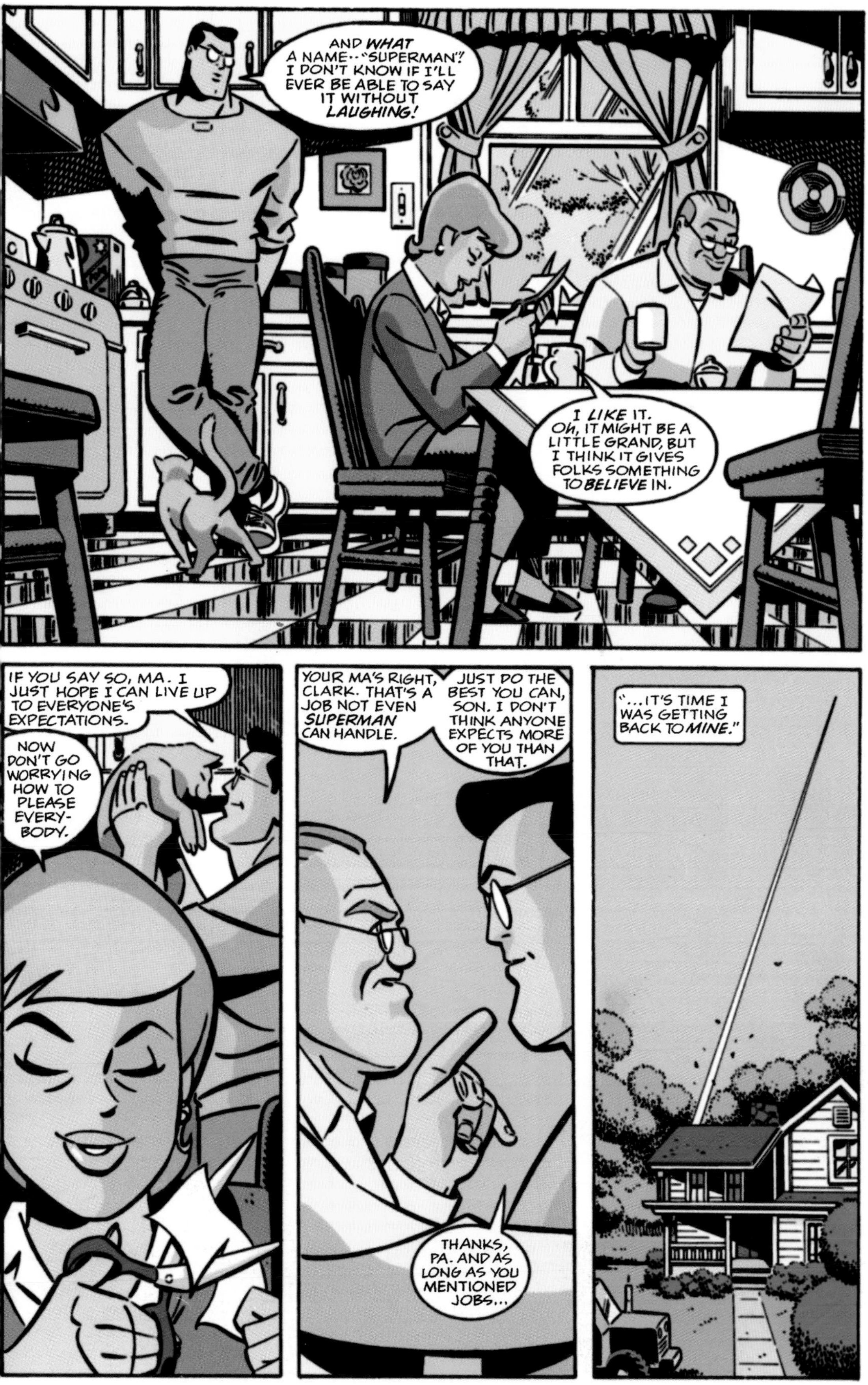
AND WHAT A NAME--"SUPERMAN"! I DON'T KNOW IF I'LL EVER BE ABLE TO SAY IT WITHOUT LAUGHING!
I LIKE IT. Oh, IT MIGHT BE A LITTLE GRAND, BUT I THINK IT GIVES FOLKS SOMETHING TO BELIEVE IN.
IF YOU SAY SO, MA. I JUST HOPE I CAN LIVE UP TO EVERYONE'S EXPECTATIONS.
NOW DON'T GO WORRYING HOW TO PLEASE EVERY-BODY.
YOUR MA'S RIGHT, CLARK. THAT'S A JOB NOT EVEN SUPERMAN CAN HANDLE.
JUST DO THE BEST YOU CAN, SON. I DON'T THINK ANYONE EXPECTS MORE OF YOU THAN THAT.
THANKS, PA. AND AS LONG AS YOU MENTIONED JOBS...
"...IT'S TIME I WAS GETTING BACK TO MINE."

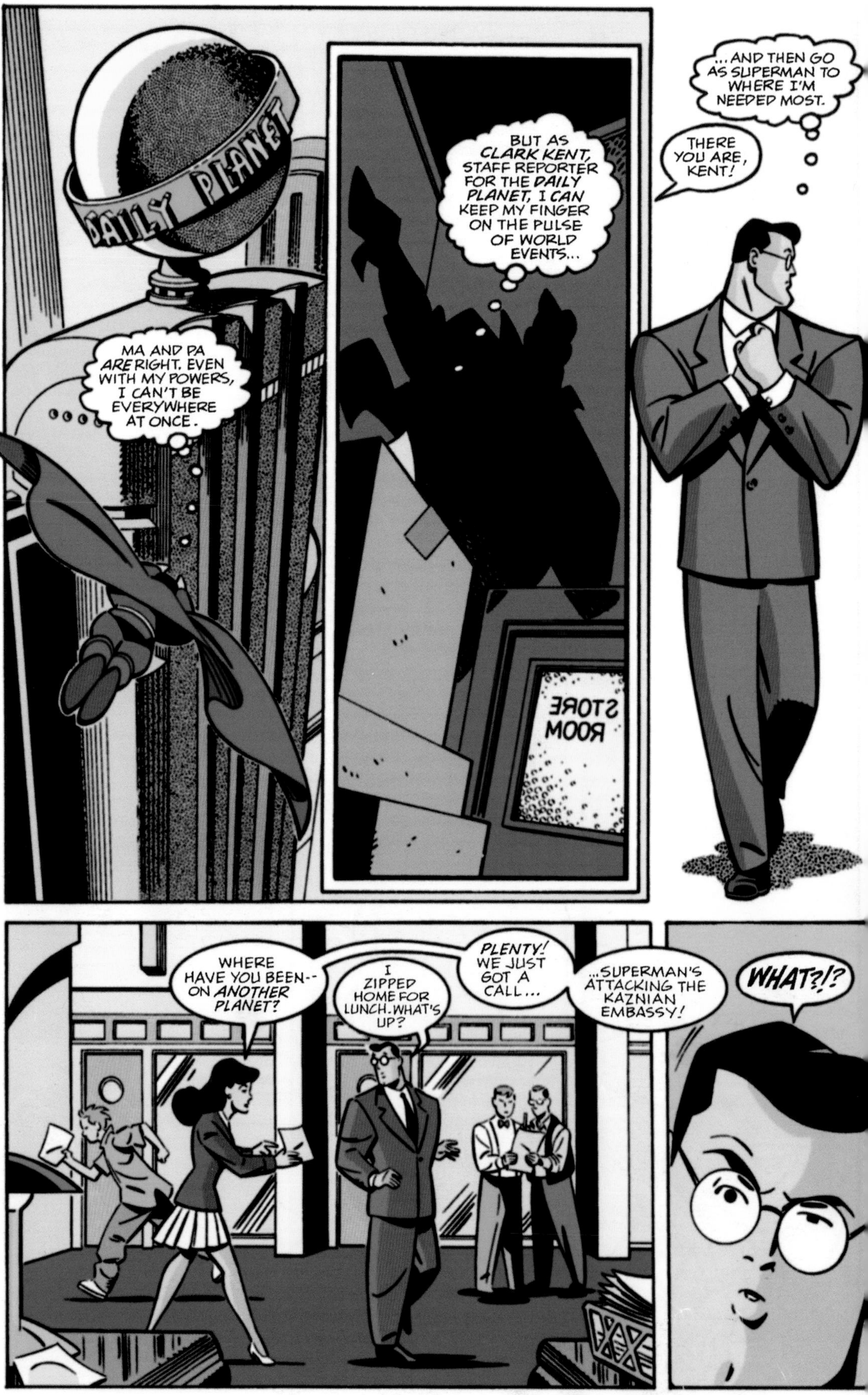

DAILY PLANET
MA AND PA ARE RIGHT. EVEN WITH MY POWERS, I CAN'T BE EVERYWHERE AT ONCE.
BUT AS CLARK KENT, STAFF REPORTER FOR THE DAILY PLANET, I CAN KEEP MY FINGER ON THE PULSE OF WORLD EVENTS...
STORE ROOM
...AND THEN GO AS SUPERMAN TO WHERE I'M NEEDED MOST.
THERE YOU ARE, KENT!
WHERE HAVE YOU BEEN--ON ANOTHER PLANET?
I ZIPPED HOME FOR LUNCH. WHAT'S UP?
PLENTY! WE JUST GOT A CALL...
...SUPERMAN'S ATTACKING THE KAZNIAN EMBASSY!
WHAT?!?

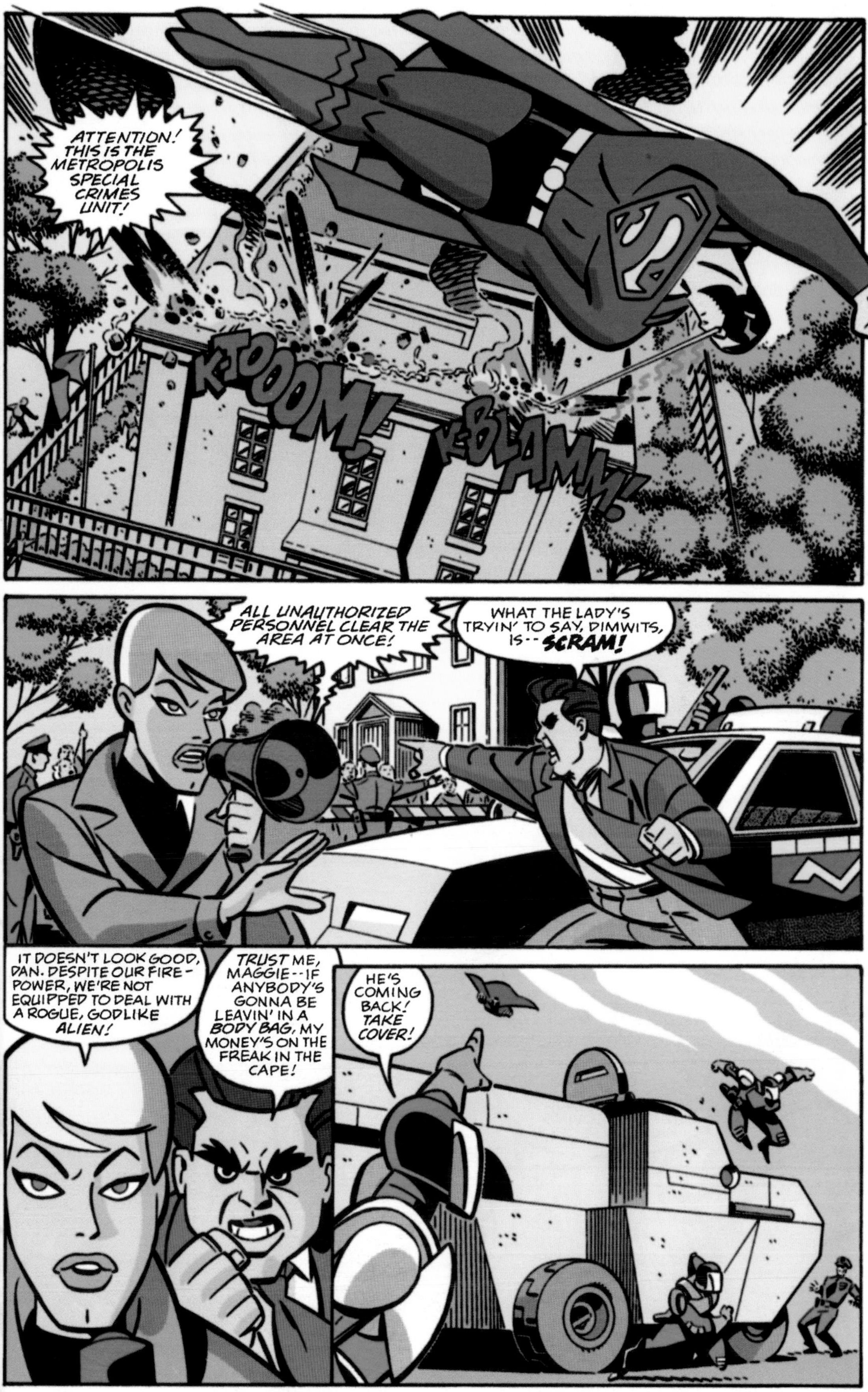
ATTENTION! THIS IS THE METROPOLIS SPECIAL CRIMES UNIT!
K-TOOOOM!
K-BLAMM!
ALL UNAUTHORIZED PERSONNEL CLEAR THE AREA AT ONCE!
WHAT THE LADY'S TRYIN' TO SAY, DIMWITS, IS-- SCRAM!
IT DOESN'T LOOK GOOD, DAN. DESPITE OUR FIRE-POWER, WE'RE NOT EQUIPPED TO DEAL WITH A ROGUE, GODLIKE ALIEN!
TRUST ME, MAGGIE--IF ANYBODY'S GONNA BE LEAVIN' IN A BODY BAG, MY MONEY'S ON THE FREAK IN THE CAPE!
HE'S COMING BACK! TAKE COVER!

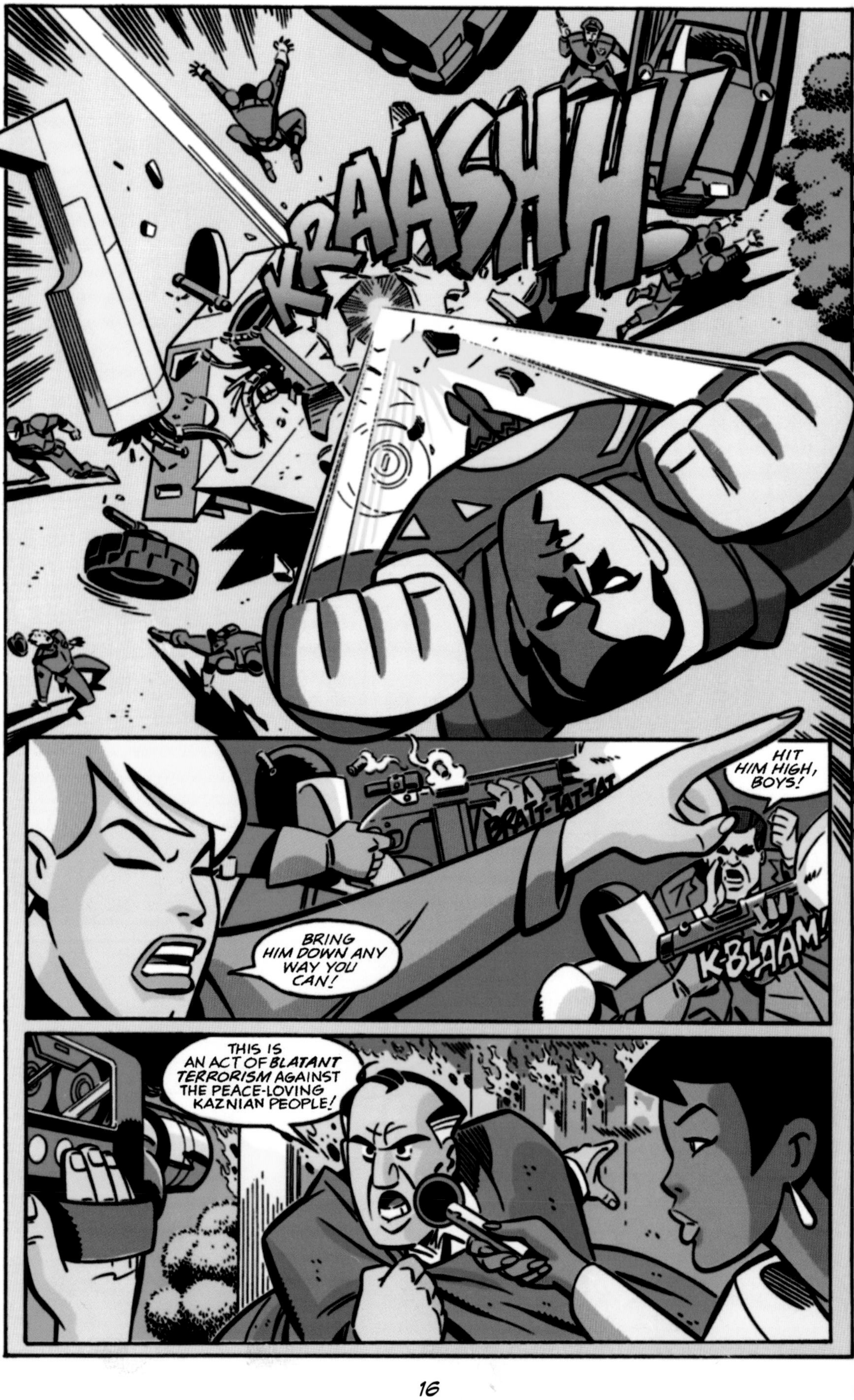
KRAASHH!!
HIT HIM HIGH, BOYS!
BRATT-TAT-TAT
BRING HIM DOWN ANY WAY YOU CAN!
K-BLAAM!
THIS IS AN ACT OF BLATANT TERRORISM AGAINST THE PEACE-LOVING KAZNIAN PEOPLE!

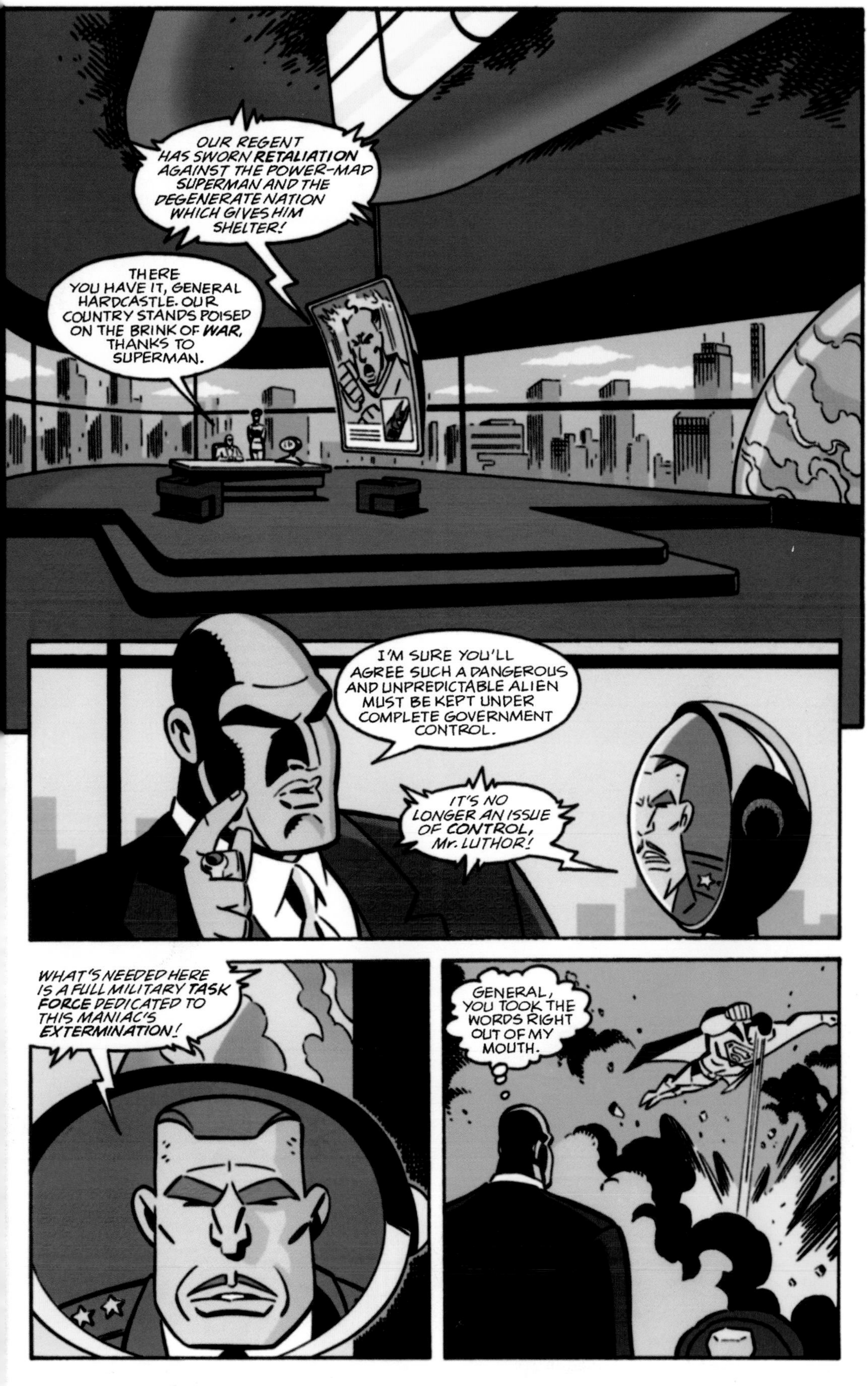
OUR REGENT HAS SWORN RETALIATION AGAINST THE POWER-MAD SUPERMAN AND THE DEGENERATE NATION WHICH GIVES HIM SHELTER!
THERE YOU HAVE IT, GENERAL HARDCASTLE. OUR COUNTRY STANDS POISED ON THE BRINK OF WAR, THANKS TO SUPERMAN.
I'M SURE YOU'LL AGREE SUCH A DANGEROUS AND UNPREDICTABLE ALIEN MUST BE KEPT UNDER COMPLETE GOVERNMENT CONTROL.
IT'S NO LONGER AN ISSUE OF CONTROL, Mr. LUTHOR!
WHAT'S NEEDED HERE IS A FULL MILITARY TASK FORCE DEDICATED TO THIS MANIAC'S EXTERMINATION!
GENERAL, YOU TOOK THE WORDS RIGHT OUT OF MY MOUTH.

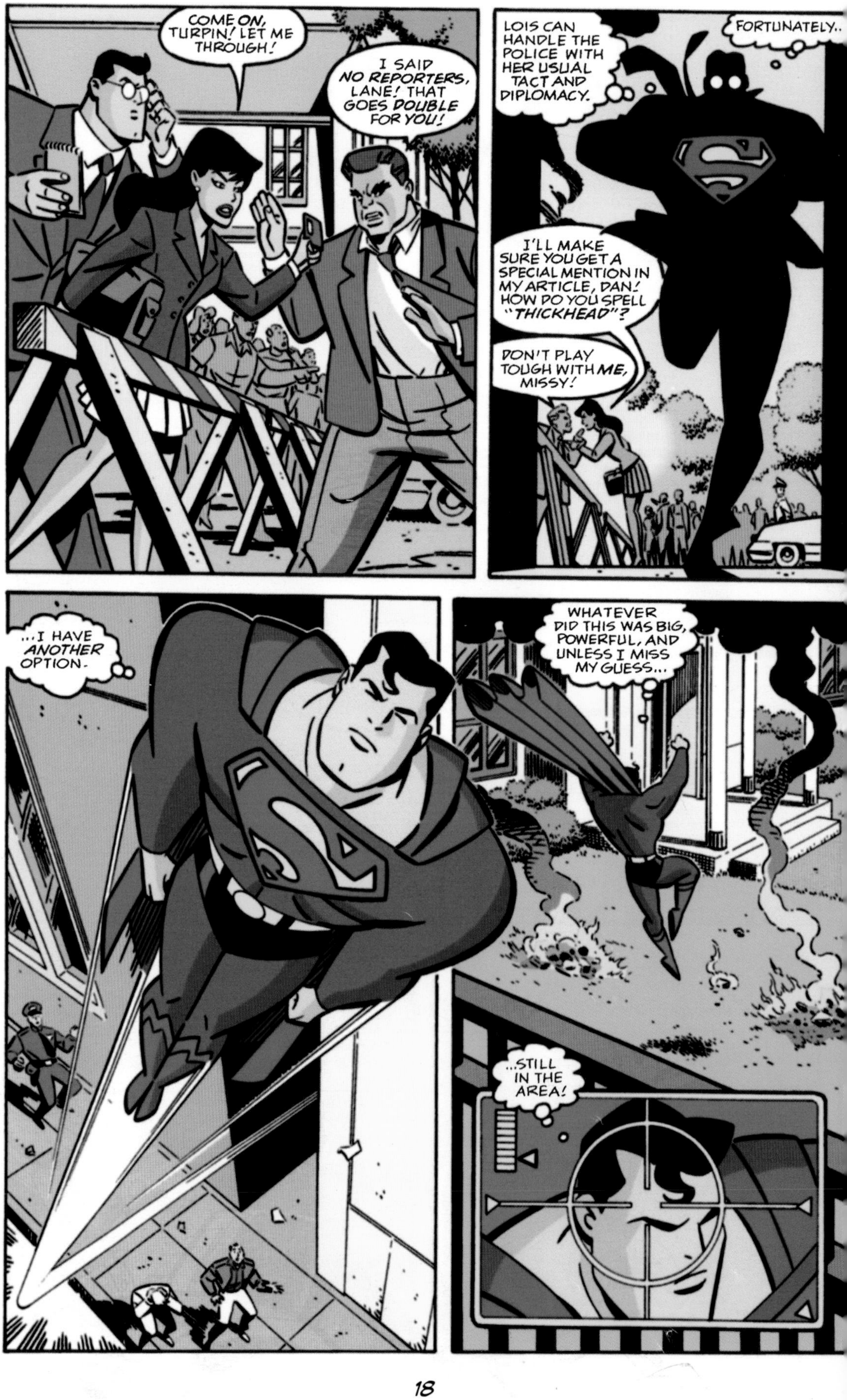
COME ON, TURPIN! LET ME THROUGH!
I SAID NO REPORTERS, LANE! THAT GOES DOUBLE FOR YOU!
LOIS CAN HANDLE THE POLICE WITH HER USUAL TACT AND DIPLOMACY.
FORTUNATELY..
I'LL MAKE SURE YOU GET A SPECIAL MENTION IN MY ARTICLE, DAN! HOW DO YOU SPELL "THICKHEAD"?
DON'T PLAY TOUGH WITH ME, MISSY!
...I HAVE ANOTHER OPTION.
WHATEVER DID THIS WAS BIG, POWERFUL, AND UNLESS I MISS MY GUESS...
...STILL IN THE AREA!

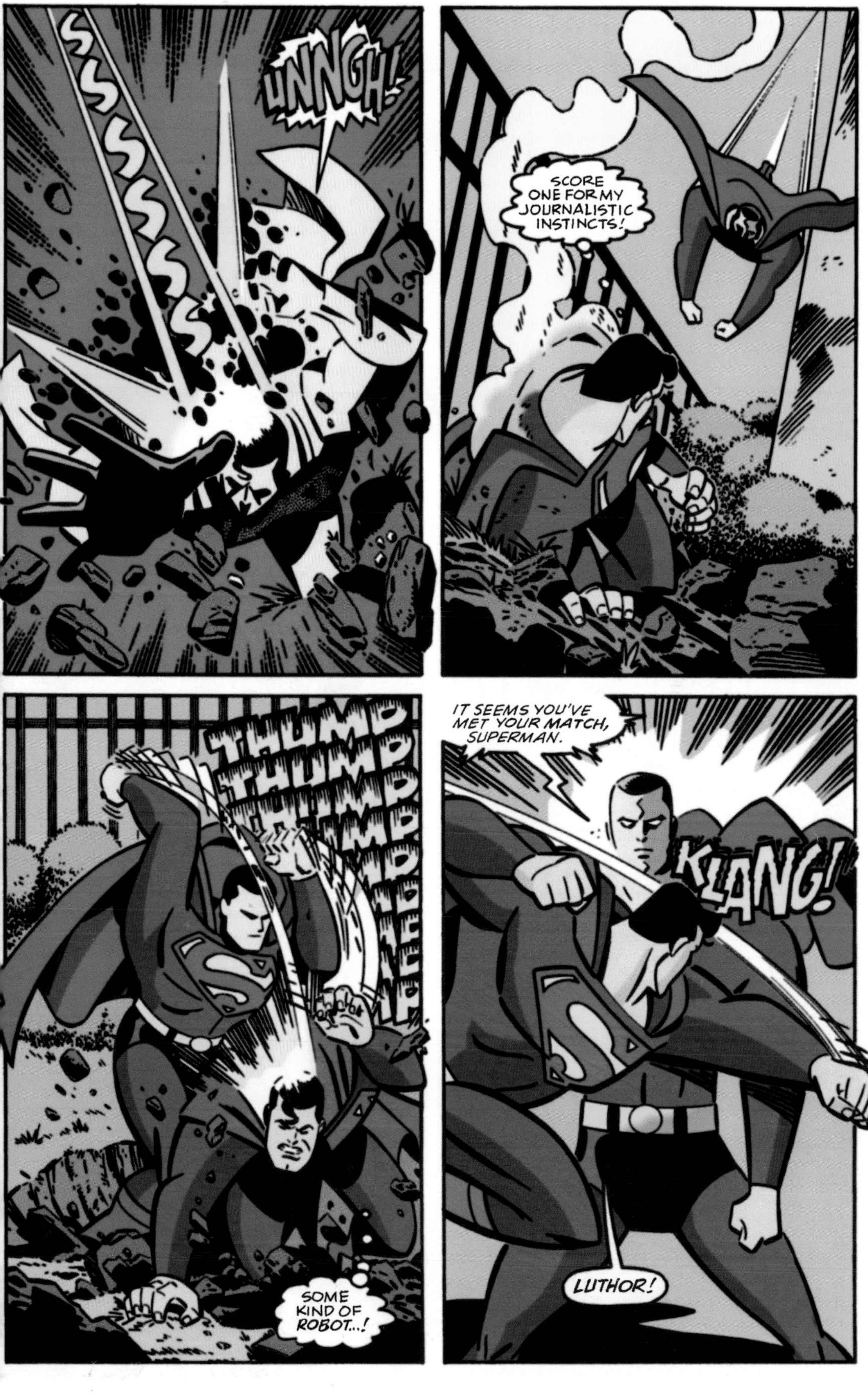
SSSSSS
UNNGH!
SCORE ONE FOR MY JOURNALISTIC INSTINCTS!
THUMP THUMP THUMP THUMP THUMP
SOME KIND OF ROBOT...!
IT SEEMS YOU'VE MET YOUR MATCH, SUPERMAN.
KLANG!
LUTHOR!

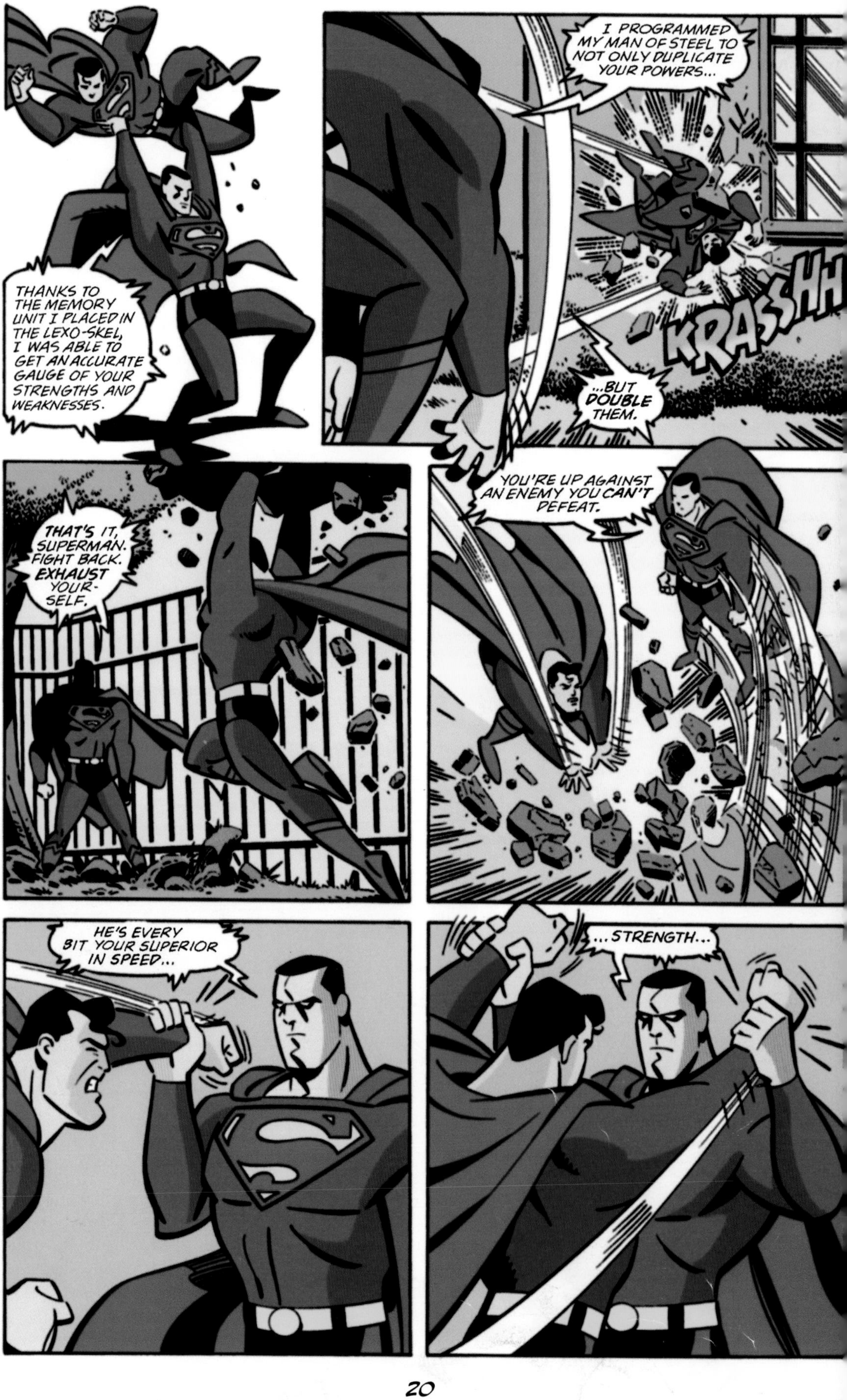
THANKS TO THE MEMORY UNIT I PLACED IN THE LEXO-SKEL, I WAS ABLE TO GET AN ACCURATE GAUGE OF YOUR STRENGTHS AND WEAKNESSES.
I PROGRAMMED MY MAN OF STEEL TO NOT ONLY DUPLICATE YOUR POWERS...
KRASSHH
...BUT DOUBLE THEM.
THAT'S IT, SUPERMAN. FIGHT BACK. EXHAUST YOURSELF.
YOU'RE UP AGAINST AN ENEMY YOU CAN'T DEFEAT.
HE'S EVERY BIT YOUR SUPERIOR IN SPEED...
...STRENGTH...

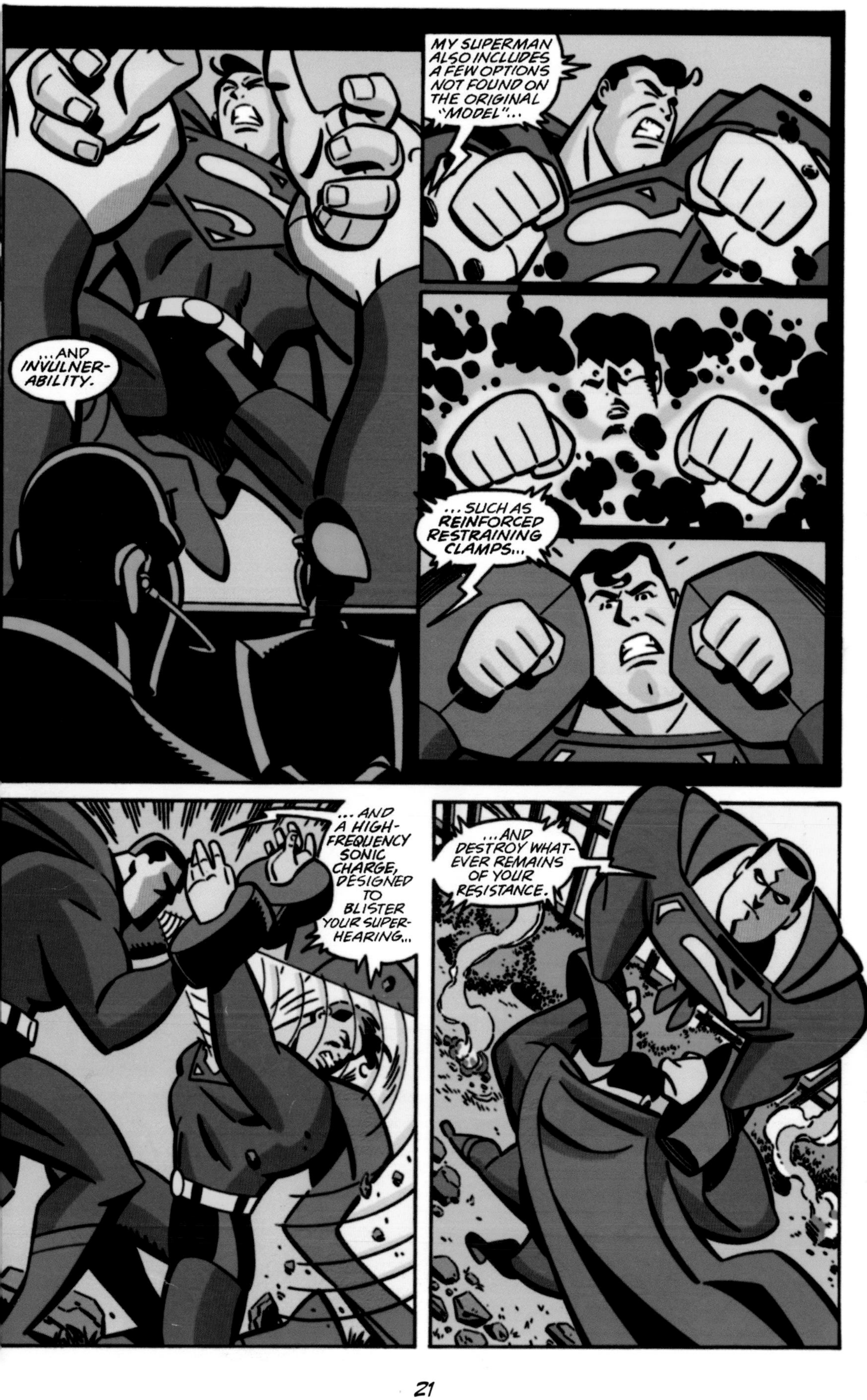
...AND INVULNER-ABILITY.
MY SUPERMAN ALSO INCLUDES A FEW OPTIONS NOT FOUND ON THE ORIGINAL "MODEL"...
...SUCH AS REINFORCED RESTRAINING CLAMPS...
...AND A HIGH-FREQUENCY SONIC CHARGE, DESIGNED TO BLISTER YOUR SUPER-HEARING...
...AND DESTROY WHAT-EVER REMAINS OF YOUR RESISTANCE.

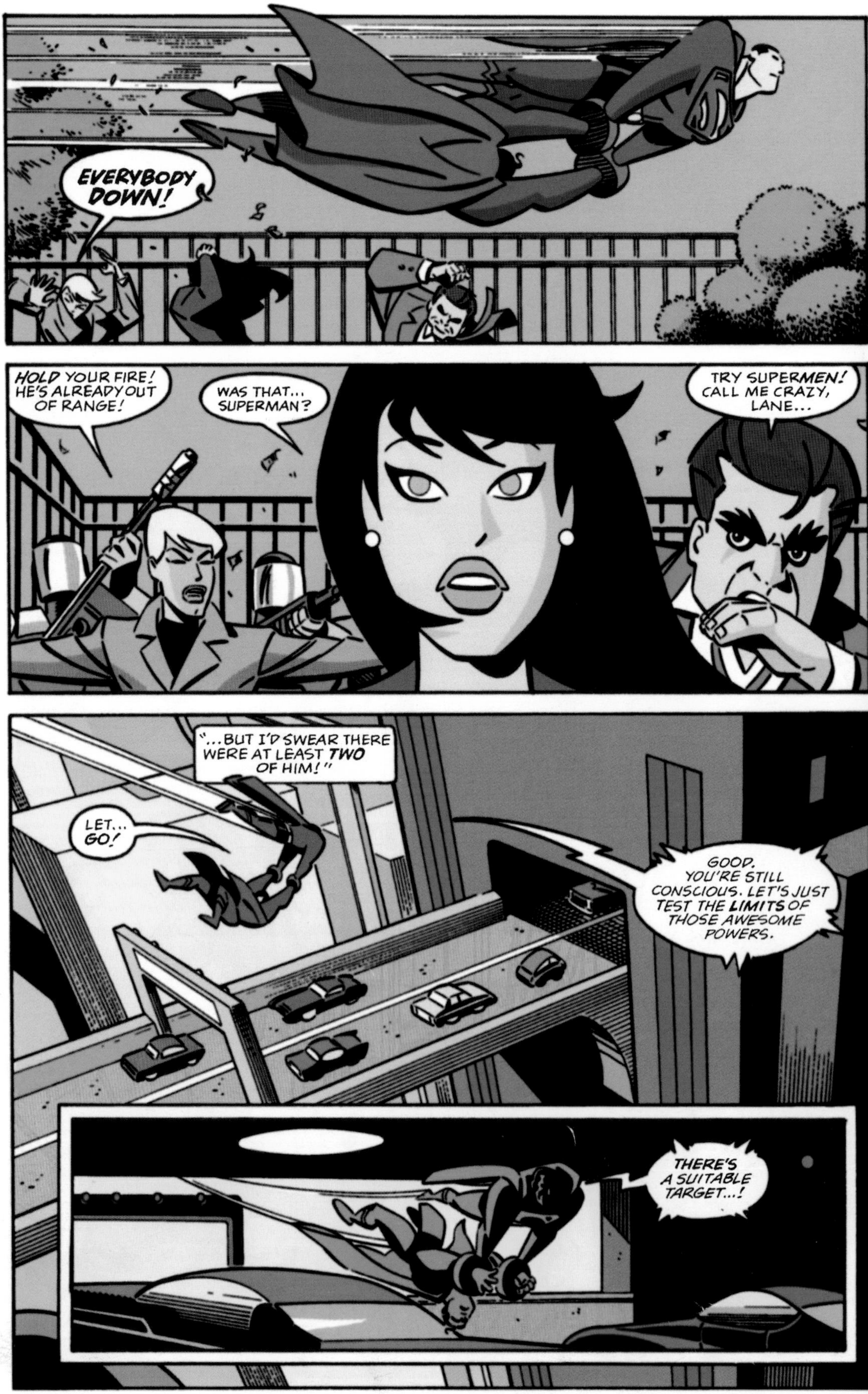
EVERYBODY DOWN!
HOLD YOUR FIRE! HE'S ALREADY OUT OF RANGE!
WAS THAT... SUPERMAN?
TRY SUPERMEN! CALL ME CRAZY, LANE...
"...BUT I'D SWEAR THERE WERE AT LEAST TWO OF HIM!"
LET... GO!
GOOD. YOU'RE STILL CONSCIOUS. LET'S JUST TEST THE LIMITS OF THOSE AWESOME POWERS.
THERE'S A SUITABLE TARGET...!

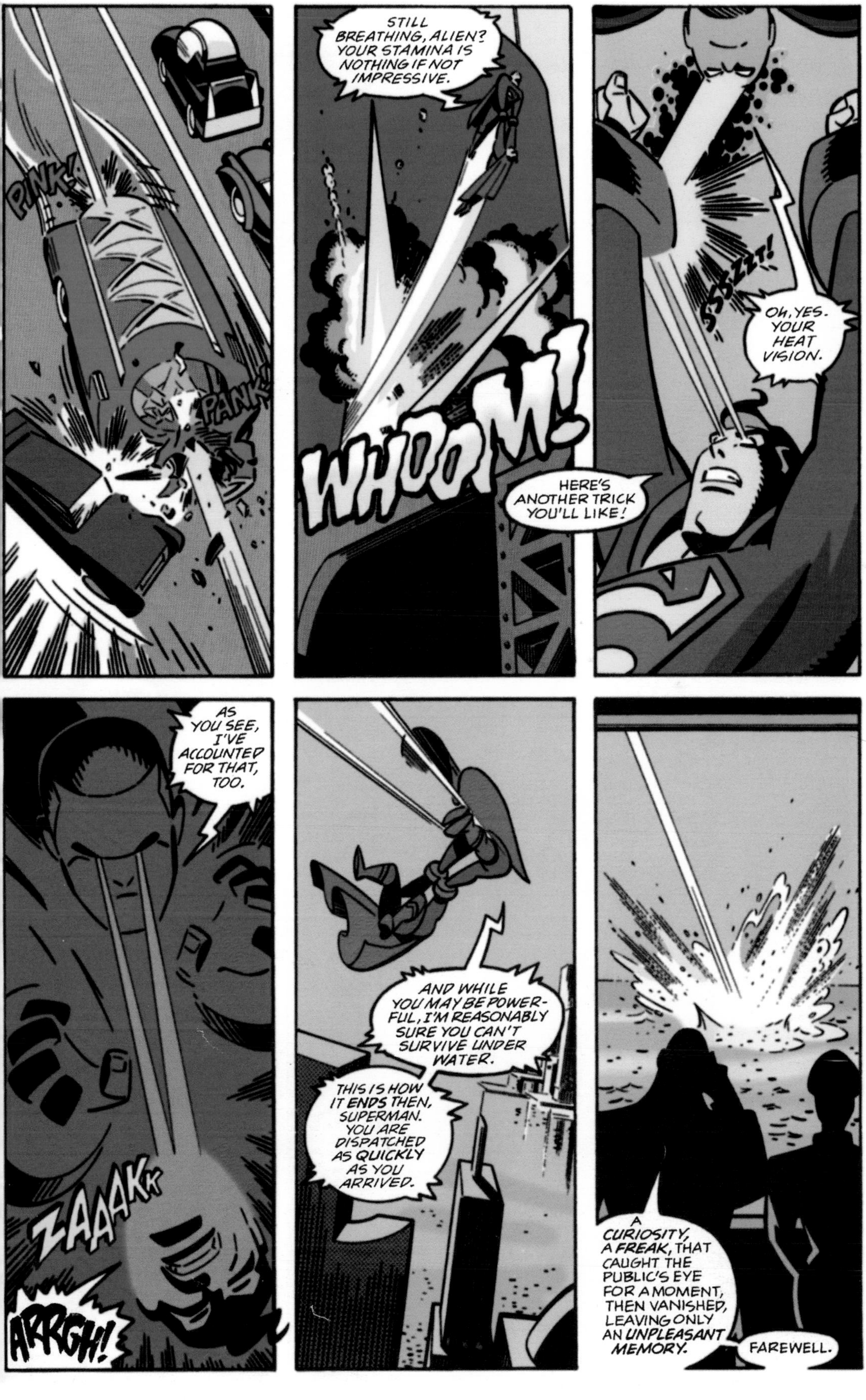
PINK!
PANK!
STILL BREATHING, ALIEN? YOUR STAMINA IS NOTHING IF NOT IMPRESSIVE.
WHOOM!
HERE'S ANOTHER TRICK YOU'LL LIKE!
SSSZZT!
Oh, YES. YOUR HEAT VISION.
AS YOU SEE, I'VE ACCOUNTED FOR THAT, TOO.
ZAAAKK
ARRGH!
AND WHILE YOU MAY BE POWER-FUL, I'M REASONABLY SURE YOU CAN'T SURVIVE UNDER WATER.
THIS IS HOW IT ENDS THEN, SUPERMAN. YOU ARE DISPATCHED AS QUICKLY AS YOU ARRIVED.
A CURIOSITY, A FREAK, THAT CAUGHT THE PUBLIC'S EYE FOR A MOMENT, THEN VANISHED, LEAVING ONLY AN UNPLEASANT MEMORY.
FAREWELL.

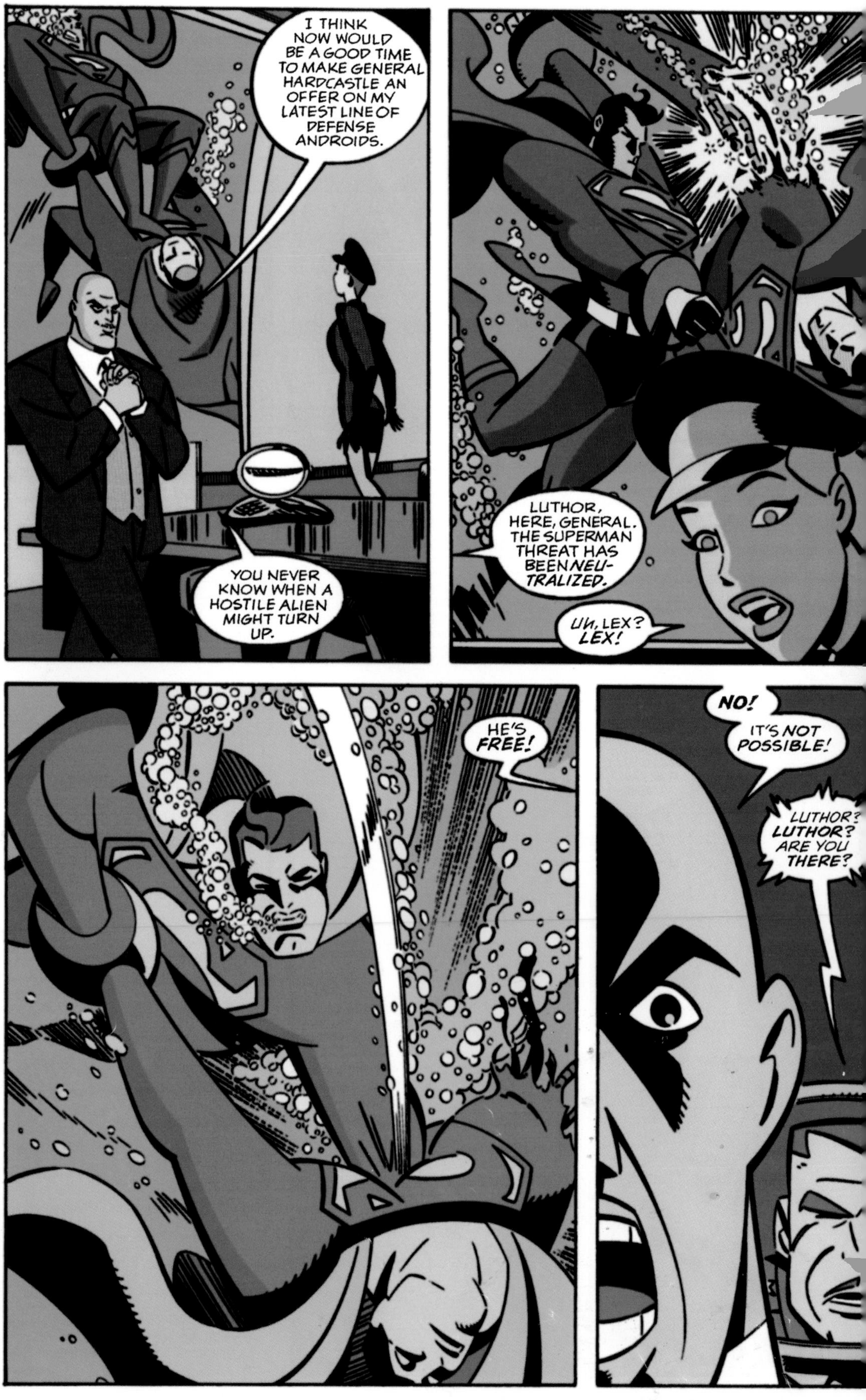
I THINK NOW WOULD BE A GOOD TIME TO MAKE GENERAL HARDCASTLE AN OFFER ON MY LATEST LINE OF DEFENSE ANDROIDS.
YOU NEVER KNOW WHEN A HOSTILE ALIEN MIGHT TURN UP.
LUTHOR, HERE, GENERAL. THE SUPERMAN THREAT HAS BEEN NEUTRALIZED.
UH, LEX? LEX!
HE'S FREE!
NO!
IT'S NOT POSSIBLE!
LUTHOR? LUTHOR? ARE YOU THERE?

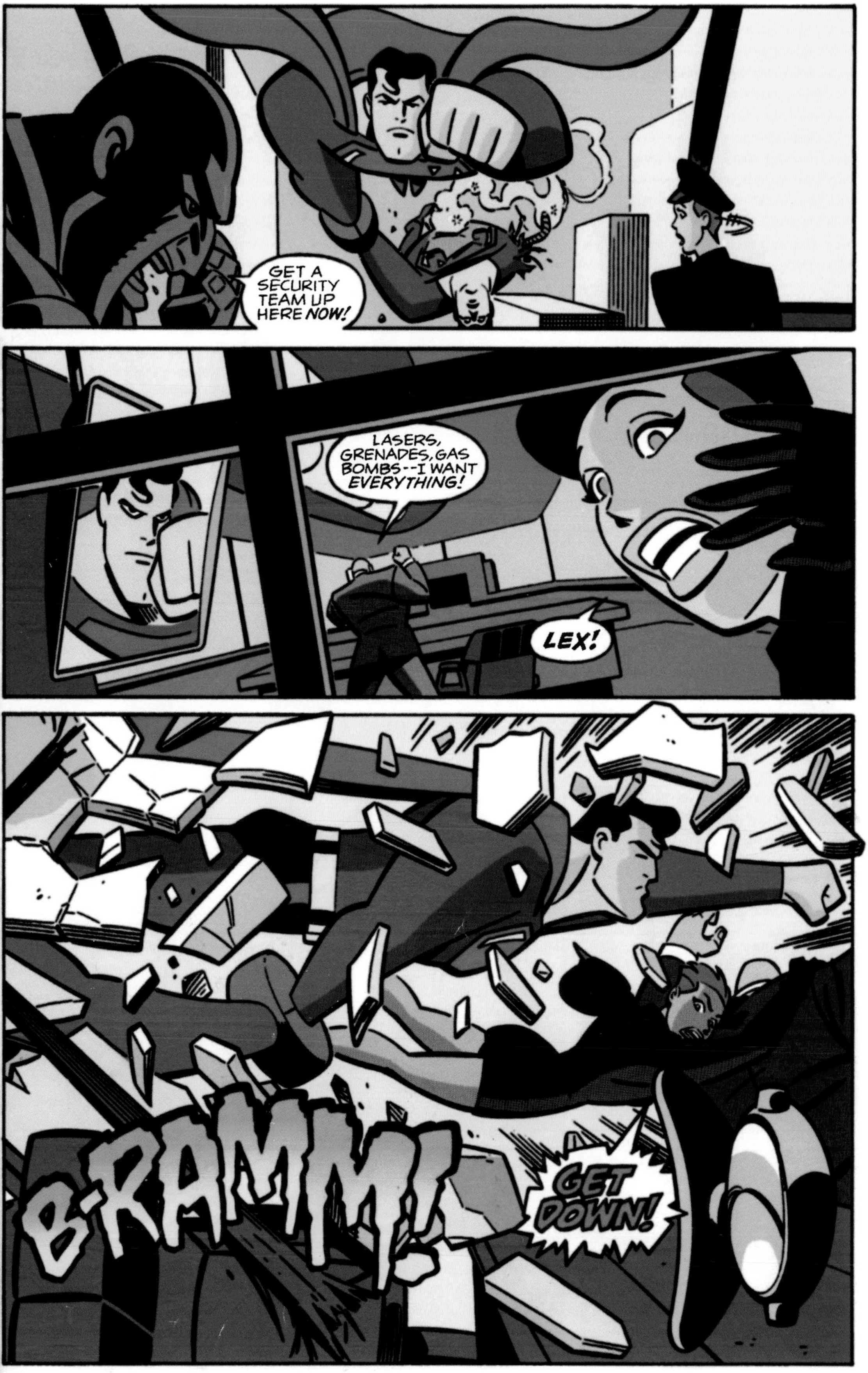
GET A SECURITY TEAM UP HERE NOW!
LASERS, GRENADES, GAS BOMBS--I WANT EVERYTHING!
LEX!
B-RAMM!
GET DOWN!

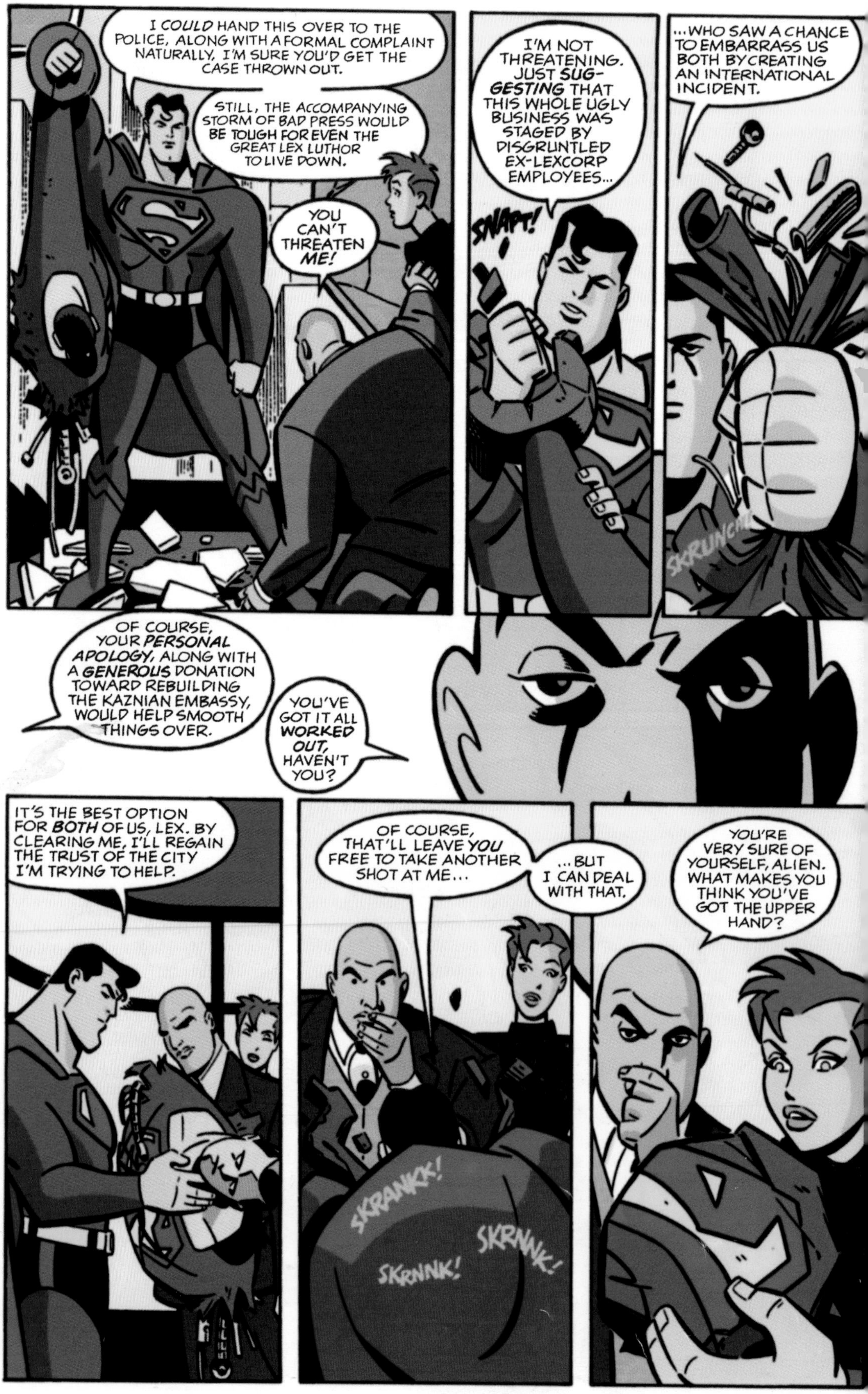

I COULD HAND THIS OVER TO THE POLICE, ALONG WITH A FORMAL COMPLAINT NATURALLY, I'M SURE YOU'D GET THE CASE THROWN OUT.
STILL, THE ACCOMPANYING STORM OF BAD PRESS WOULD BE TOUGH FOR EVEN THE GREAT LEX LUTHOR TO LIVE DOWN.
YOU CAN'T THREATEN ME!
I'M NOT THREATENING. JUST SUG-GESTING THAT THIS WHOLE UGLY BUSINESS WAS STAGED BY DISGRUNTLED EX-LEXCORP EMPLOYEES...
SNAP!
...WHO SAW A CHANCE TO EMBARRASS US BOTH BY CREATING AN INTERNATIONAL INCIDENT.
SKRUNCH!
OF COURSE, YOUR PERSONAL APOLOGY, ALONG WITH A GENEROUS DONATION TOWARD REBUILDING THE KAZNIAN EMBASSY, WOULD HELP SMOOTH THINGS OVER.
YOU'VE GOT IT ALL WORKED OUT, HAVEN'T YOU?
IT'S THE BEST OPTION FOR BOTH OF US, LEX. BY CLEARING ME, I'LL REGAIN THE TRUST OF THE CITY I'M TRYING TO HELP.
OF COURSE, THAT'LL LEAVE YOU FREE TO TAKE ANOTHER SHOT AT ME...
...BUT I CAN DEAL WITH THAT.
SKRANKK!
SKRNNK!
SKRNNK!
YOU'RE VERY SURE OF YOURSELF, ALIEN. WHAT MAKES YOU THINK YOU'VE GOT THE UPPER HAND?

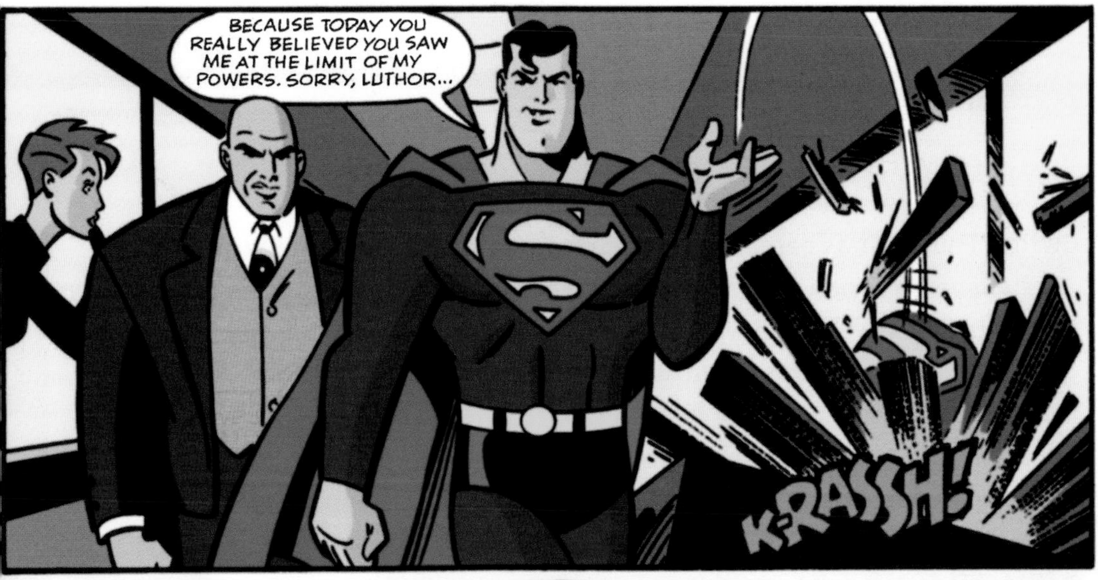
BECAUSE TODAY YOU REALLY BELIEVED YOU SAW ME AT THE LIMIT OF MY POWERS. SORRY, LUTHOR...
K-RASSH!

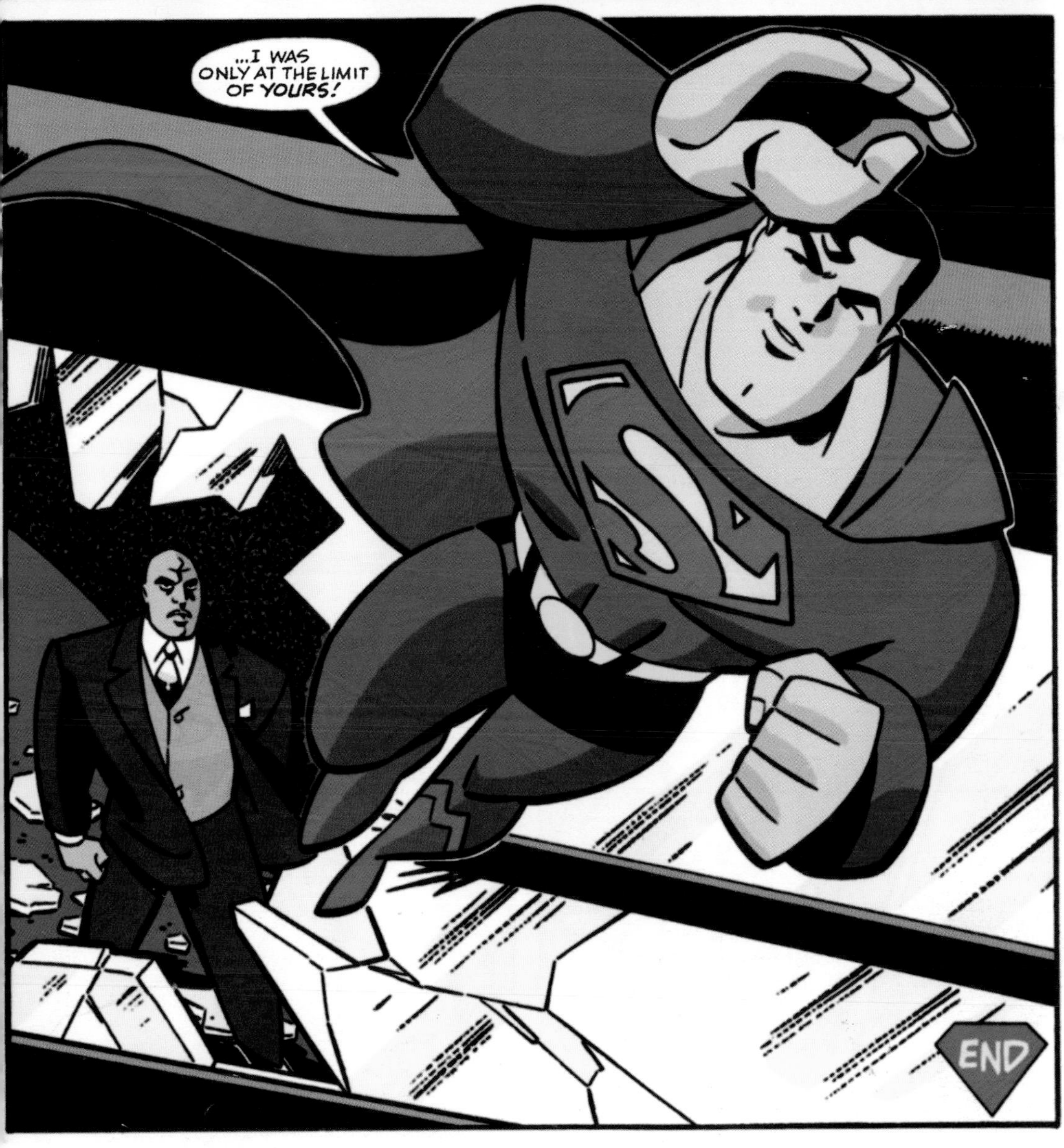
...I WAS ONLY AT THE LIMIT OF YOURS!
END

CREATORS

PAUL DINI WRITER

Writer Paul Dini has earned five Emmy Awards for his work on *Batman: The Animated Series*, *Superman: The Animated Series*, and *Justice League Unlimited*. His live-action work includes story editing for *Lost*. In comics, his *Batman Adventures: Mad Love*, with artist Bruce Timm, won numerous awards. In 2006, he was head writer for DC's *Countdown to Infinite Crisis* and took over Batman's adventures in *Detective Comics*. More recently, he wrote the Batman-based series *Gotham City Sirens* and *Batman: Streets of Gotham*.

RICK BURCHETT PENCILLER

Rick Burchett has worked as a comics artist for more than 25 years. He has received the comics industry's Eisner Award three times, Spain's Haxtur Award, and he has been nominated for England's Eagle Award. Rick lives with his wife and two sons near St. Louis, Missouri.

TERRY AUSTIN INKER

Throughout his career, inker Terry Austin has received dozens of awards for his work on high-profile comics for DC Comics and Marvel, such as *The Uncanny X-Men*, *Doctor Strange*, *Justice League America*, *Green Lantern*, and *Superman Adventures.* He lives near Poughkeepsie, New York.

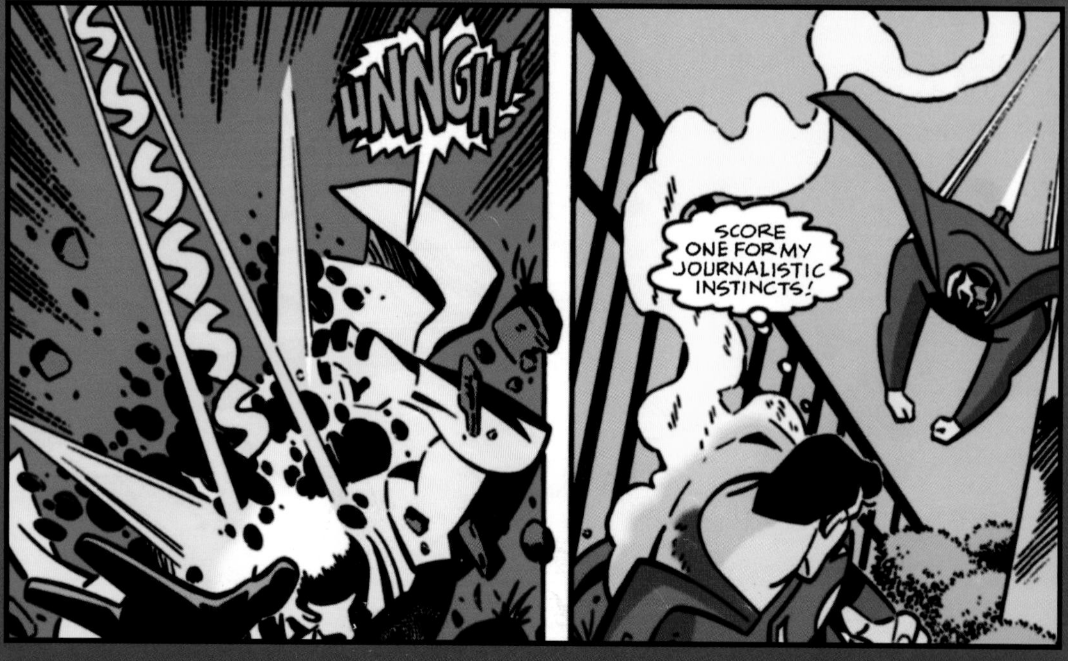
SSSSSS
UNNGH!
SCORE ONE FOR MY JOURNALISTIC INSTINCTS!

GLOSSARY

blatant (BLAY-tuhnt)--obvious and shameless

cynic (SIN-ik)--a person who believes that selfishness is the primary motivation for people

degenerate (di-GEN-uh-rate)--to become worse or inferior in quality, or a person who is immoral or a criminal

dissent (di-SENT)--disagreement with an idea or opinion

duplicate (DOO-pluh-kate)--a copy, or double

exclusive (ek-SKLOO-siv)--a story that appears in one place only

extermination (ek-stur-muh-NAY-shuhn)--the killing of large amounts of people or animals

fortunate (FOR-chuh-nit)--lucky

hostile (HOSS-tuhl)--unfriendly or angry

inflicts (in-FLIKZ)--causes suffering to someone or something

potent (POHT-uhnt)--powerful or strong

retaliation (ri-TAL-ee-ay-shuhn)--an act of revenge

salvage (SAL-vij)--to rescue property from a shipwreck, fire, or other disaster

simulate (SIM-yoo-late)--pretend or fake

SUPERMAN GLOSSARY

Clark Kent: Superman's alter ego, Clark Kent, is a reporter for the *Daily Planet* newspaper and was raised by Ma and Pa Kent. No one knows he is Superman except for his adopted parents, the Kents.

The Daily Planet: the city of Metropolis's biggest and most read newspaper. Clark, Lois, Jimmy, and Perry all work for the *Daily Planet*.

Invulnerability: Superman's invulnerability makes him impervious to harm. Almost nothing can hurt him -- except for Kryptonite, a radioactive rock from his home planet, Krypton.

Jimmy Olsen: Jimmy is a cub reporter and photographer. He is also a friend to Lois and Clark.

The Kent Family: Ma and Pa Kent found Superman when he crashed to Earth from his home planet, Krypton. They raised him as their own child, giving him the name Clark.

Lex Luthor: Lex believes Superman is a threat to Earth and must be stopped. He will do anything it takes to bring the Man of Steel to his knees.

Lois Lane: like Clark Kent, Lois is a reporter at the *Daily Planet*. She is also one of Clark's best friends.

Metropolis: the city where Clark Kent (Superman) lives.

Perry White: Clark's boss at the *Daily Planet* newspaper. He has a temper and can be very impatient sometimes.

VISUAL QUESTIONS & PROMPTS

1. In this panel, Clark Kent pretends to not know Superman. Why do you think it's important for him to keep his other identity a secret? Explain your answer.

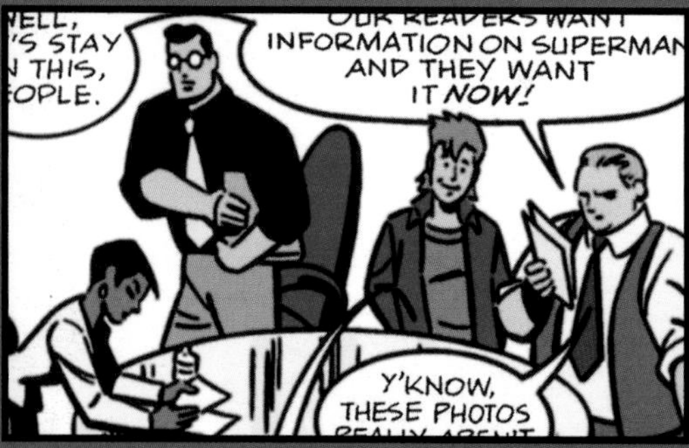

INFORMATION ON SUPERMAN AND THEY WANT IT NOW!
Y'KNOW, THESE PHOTOS

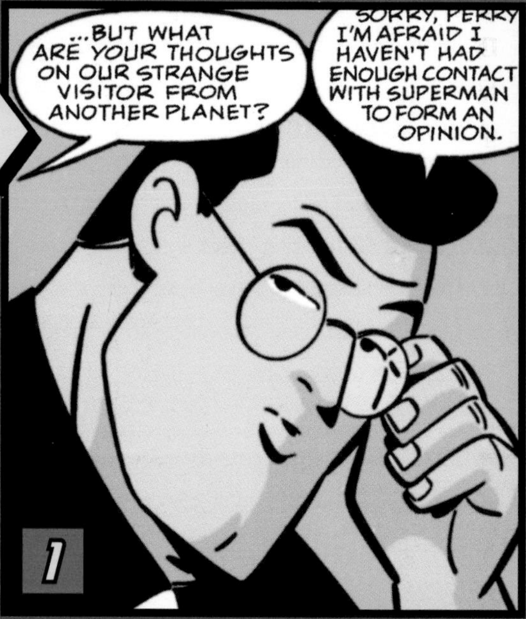

...BUT WHAT ARE YOUR THOUGHTS ON OUR STRANGE VISITOR FROM ANOTHER PLANET?
SORRY, PERRY I'M AFRAID I HAVEN'T HAD ENOUGH CONTACT WITH SUPERMAN TO FORM AN OPINION.
1

2. The woman in the black outfit is Mercy Graves, an employee of Lex Luthor's. Based on the panel below, what role do you think she plays in his company? Explain.

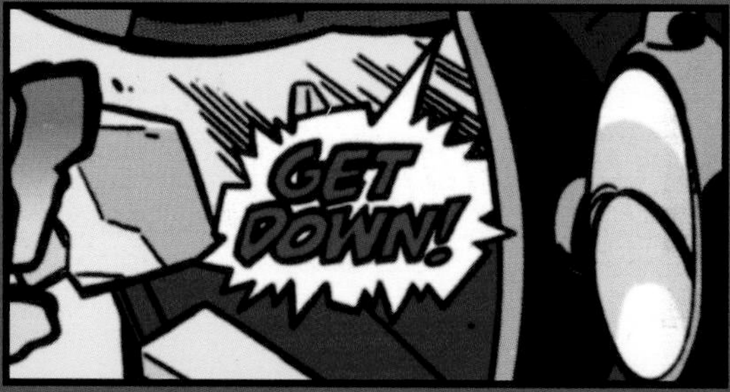

GET DOWN!

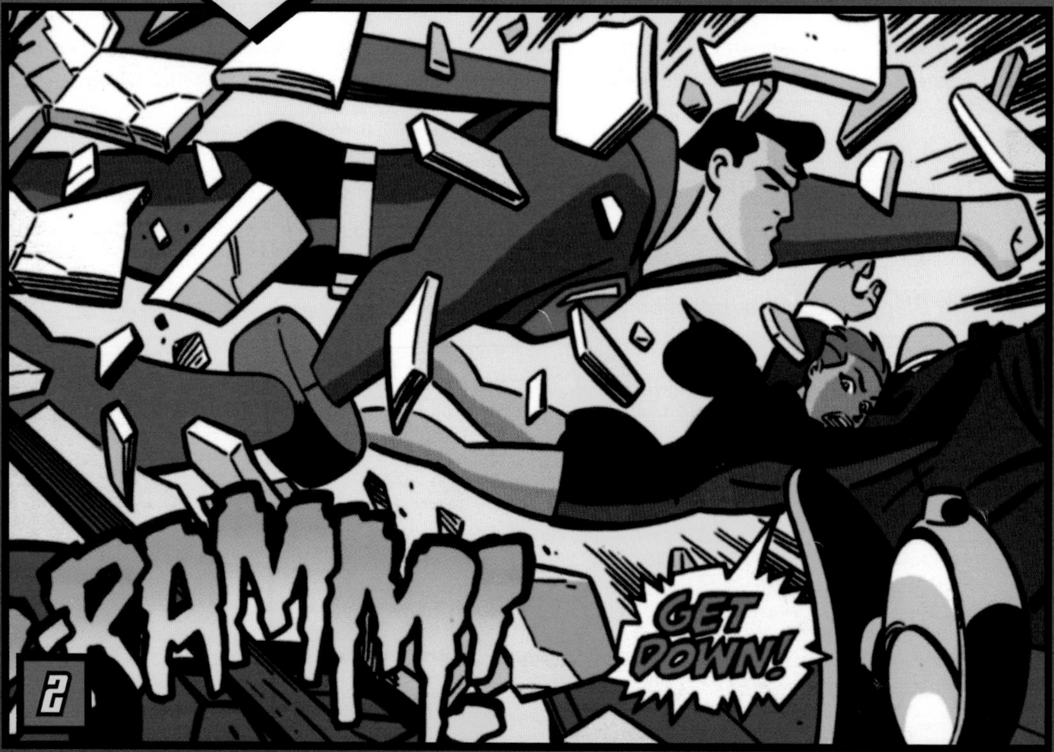

RAMM!
GET DOWN!
2

3. What do you think Lex's motivations are for getting rid of Superman? Is he concerned for Metropolis? Does he want to get rid of his competition? Explain your answer by referencing specific panels in this book.

...OR FOR INSTANCE.

METROPOLIS WAS *NOTHING* UNTIL I REBUILT IT ACCORDING TO MY VISION. NOW MOST OF ITS PEOPLE WORK FOR LEXCORP OR ONE OF ITS MANY SUBSIDIARIES, AND THE CITY'S FEW VOICES OF DISSENT, SUCH AS *S.T.A.R. LABS* AND THE *DAILY PLANET*, ARE ALLOWED TO EXIST SIMPLY BECAUSE THEY *AMUSE* ME.

ALL IN ALL, IT'S A PERFECT PICTURE OF ORDER.

3 ...SUPERMAN ...SENTS A *THREAT* TO ...RDER. HE COULD ...E PEOPLE, MAKE ...CERTAIN OF WHO ...EALLY HAS THEIR BEST INTER-

4. Of all Superman's skills, which ones turned out to be the most helpful in this book? If you could have any of Superman's superpowers, which one would you want? Why would you choose that power?

SSZZT!

OH, YES. YOUR HEAT VISION.

...'S ...RICK ...KE!

4

Whoosh!

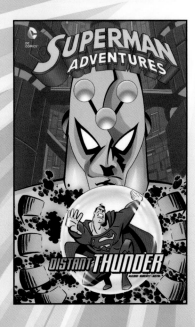